NN C

....

My Nasty Neighbours

'I laughed so much I got the hiccups'
THE IRISH TIMES

'Full marks for originality and readability'
BOOKS IRELAND

'Such an enjoyable read ...
hilarious one-liners'
CHILDREN'S BOOKS IN IRELAND

WHAT THEY SAID ABOUT *Cherokee*

'Original, beautifully fresh'
ROBERT DUNBAR, CHILDREN'S BOOKS IN IRELAND

'A major find'
BOOKS IRELAND

Creina Mansfield has a Master's degree in novel writing from Manchester University. She has written *My Nutty Neighbours*, a sequel to this book; *Cherokee*, a novel about a young boy and his grandfather who both love to play jazz; *Fairchild*; and, for younger readers, *Snip, Snip!* in which a little obsession with scissors leads to interesting situations.

To Bob, with love

My Nasty Neighbours

Creina Mansfield

THE O'BRIEN PRESS
DUBLIN

First published 1995 by The O'Brien Press Ltd.,
20 Victoria Road, Dublin 6, Ireland.
Reprinted 1997, 1998, 2006.

British Library Cataloguing-in-publication Data
Mansfield, Creina
My nasty neighbours
1.Parent and teenager - Juvenile fiction 2.Children's stories
I.Title
823.9'14[J]

4 5 6 7 8 9 10
06 07 08 09 10

ISBN-10 0-86278-462-X
ISBN-13 978-0-86278-462-1

The O'Brien receives
assistance from

arts
council
chomhairle
ealaíon

Editing, typesetting, layout and design: The O'Brien Press Ltd
Cover illustration: Kate Sheppard
Printing: Cox & Wyman Ltd

Contents

CHAPTER ONE

Happy Families

There should be a law against people talking to you when you're trying to watch TV.

I'd just settled on my sofa when Mum began. 'David, I have a distinct memory that twelve years ago I taught you to walk! All you seem to do nowadays is lie on that sofa and gawp at the television set.'

Notice that word 'gawp'. I gawp; you watch; they *view*. Mum was rattled, and I wasn't going to get any peace.

I patted the cushions around me. I like six for complete comfort – three under my head, one under my left elbow and two propping up my feet.

'I'm just relaxing,' I pointed out reasonably. 'I am allowed to relax, aren't I?' There is no point sitting up to watch television when you can lie down.

And I was just in from rugby practice so it wasn't as if I hadn't had any exercise. Take it from me, I am definitely the fittest member of the Stirling family, made up of Mum, Dad, my brother Ian, and sister Helen and myself! Mum and Dad look like Tweedledum and Tweedledee. Ian's the original eight-stone weakling and although Helen makes a big deal about keeping fit – she puts on a leotard, trainers and a sweat-band to lift three-pound weights – I can still pick her up and put her on top of the wardrobe when she annoys me. At my school, St Joseph's, the three Rs aren't Reading, 'Riting and 'Rithmetic but Rugby, Rugby and Rugby. I've played since I started at St Joseph's at the age of seven and I'd just got a place on the A side.

So after lunch on that Tuesday I battled for every minute of the hour-long practice. I was thumped, winded and booted in the ribs; I deserved some peace and entertainment. I wanted to watch 'Gladiators' which I'd videoed from the previous Saturday. Mum obviously had other plans.

She padded through to the kitchen in her boat-like sheepskin slippers, still complaining, but I could tell that she was just taking it out on me for something either Helen or Ian had done. Being the youngest member of the family I'm the punch-bag for the other Stirlings to hit at. Luckily I'm also the biggest member of the family.

'What's up?' I called out, planning to follow up this sympathetic question with an order for hot buttered toast. Fortunately the roars of the 'Gladiator' audience drowned out most of Mum's moaning.

'... becoming impossible, David,' I heard, '... untidiness, lack of consideration ...'

'Any chance of a cup of tea?' I went on. Wolf was in good form. It took him just five seconds to whack his opponent off the pedestal. I wouldn't mind having a go at that, preferably with Ian as my opponent.

There was a time when Ian had seemed perfect. He's blond and when he was a kid he had the angelic sort of looks that adults like. A fresh, open expression like a cherub.

And if he'd whipped out a small harp and begun playing, nobody would have been surprised. He was always musical. I can't remember a time when he wasn't playing at least two musical instruments. He was already playing the violin at four years old when I was born – and I bet he didn't even stop playing to say hello. By the age of six he was playing the piano as well. He's got a great singing voice too, so he won a scholarship to St Patrick's which has a choir for the cathedral.

By my age he had the best voice in the school, which probably meant one of the best voices in the country and he sang solo in the cathedral services. The choir even made a record with Ian singing 'Ave Maria'.

Mum and Dad always talked about him having a career in music and it looked as if they were right, but not in the way they intended.

'... chance of a cup of tea?' I repeated.

'What? What?' Mum stomped through. 'He's like a stranger,' she said. 'A hideous, intrusive stranger.'

Well, he could hardly be expected to look

like Little Lord Fauntleroy all his life, I thought, but I gave Mum a sympathetic nod and asked, 'Got any hot buttered toast?'

Mum gave me a fierce look and went back to the kitchen. But she kept on complaining, '... playing that dreadful racket all through the day when he should be studying.'

When Ian was fourteen, his voice started to break which meant he couldn't control the sounds he made and he would squeak and grunt when he was singing. Mum, Dad and the school knew this would happen eventually and anyway Ian was now playing the violin and piano brilliantly. He got top marks in his exams accompanied by comments like, 'an exceptional talent – wonderful!'

So when he asked for a drum kit for his fifteenth birthday, Mum and Dad were shocked.

'You mean you want to study percussion – in an orchestra?' Dad asked hopefully. He could boast to his fellow civil servants in the Data Protection Commission about *that*.

'No, Dad, I mean I want to play the drums – in a rock band,' Ian corrected.

'But, darling,' Mum wailed, 'You're a musician, not a drummer!'

Nevertheless Ian got his drum kit. The walls shook as he practised. It was impossible to watch television, study, do anything when Ian was playing. Our house, 11, Elm Close seemed to be suffering its own localised earthquake.

He formed a group called the Oily Rags and, as Dad put it, 'promptly started to look like one'. He wore greasy black clothes, his face became a mixture of bristles and spots and he wore a razor blade in his left ear.

'I know what I'm doing,' was Ian's usual reply to Mum and Dad's complaints that he was ruining his brilliant future.

'... thinks he's going to be a big *rock star*.' Mum's voice increased in volume as she thrust a plate of hot buttered toast into my hands.

Perhaps she was trying to drown out the noise from Ian's bedroom, where the house of Heavy Metal was tuning up, with a clash of cymbals and a drum roll.

I turned up the telly and rewound the video. I wanted to watch again that bit where Wolf hammered his opponent across the head and shoulders.

That's the great thing about TV – it lets you escape from the harsh realities of life.

CHAPTER 2

Beauty is Only Skin Deep ...

Three cups of tea later and I was heading upstairs to the loo. This was when having one bathroom and a sister like Helen became a real liability. She was training to be a beautician which meant she 'studied' things like cuticles and revised eye-lash tint.

The door was locked. I heaved my right shoulder against it and yelled over the noise of Ian's drums, 'Helen, come out! I need to go in there!'

Silence from within, apart from the slight sound of someone moving beauty products about. My eighteen-year-old sister has simple looks – long, blond hair, blue eyes and a figure like those 'Baywatch' girls. And at least she was getting qualified, and, with Mum and Dad qualifications are a must. A fully qualified contract killer would be better than an unqualified genius who played for Ireland and painted masterpieces on his day off. But Helen's career choice was still a disappointment. There'd been huge rows about it.

'You're passing up an opportunity I would have died for!' Dad kept saying. He was really clever at school, had won the Literature Prize every year, Gran kept on (and kept on) telling us – but there'd been no money for university. Now his daughter refused to go.

I hammered on the door again. 'Helen, hurry up! What are you doing in there?'

'I'm nearly finished,' came Helen's unflustered voice. She never hurried.

'Skip the last dozen products and Get Out Here!' I yelled.

About eighty products have to be applied daily. They fill our one and only bathroom and it takes so long to apply all these creams, gels, mousses, sprays and lotion that Helen's ready to start taking them off just after she's finished putting them on.

Mum called from the bottom of the stairs, 'What's going on?'

'It's Helen, Mum. She's hogging the bathroom!'

Mum came up the stairs and knocked on the door. 'Helen, show some consideration for others, please!'

'I'll be two minutes!' called Helen, sweetness itself.

'Which two minutes?' I asked gruffly. 'One minute now and another in an hour's time perhaps?'

Mum got wild and hammered on the door too, shouting, 'Beauty is only skin deep!'

The door opened and Helen glided out. As I rushed in I heard Mum interrogating Helen about her date that evening.

'Who is he? Where did you meet him? Do we know him?'

Helen remained calm until Mum asked 'Who do we know who knows him?'

'Mum! How should I know? What do you want – references?' she said sharply and slammed her bedroom door.

Mum sloped off down the stairs. 'I'm just concerned for you, darling.'

I looked into Helen's room. She was painting her nails. 'Are you going for a meal?' I asked.

She nodded.

'Where's tonight's dream date taking you?' I asked enviously. Helen specialised in boyfriends with fast cars and large wallets. So it would be somewhere with great food and Helen would eat about three carrots and one bean. Food was wasted on her. I wished we had a dog so I could persuade her boyfriends to bring back doggy bags. Silver the cat never got offered anything.

'His name's Harry, and he's choosing,' Helen answered.

'Get him to try that new place in Rathmines!' I shouted, as I headed downstairs to the kitchen. Just the thought of all that food made me feel hungry.

'What a waste!' I muttered.

Mum misunderstood me. 'Of a wonderful mind,' she added, shaking her head. 'Helen got the second highest marks ever in Ireland in her Leaving Cert Latin exam,' she told me. '*Ever*,' she stressed. 'In the whole country.'

I took a packet of biscuits. 'Yup! Remind me to tell Harry that when he turns up,' I said, heading back to my TV. 'That'll impress him.'

. . . and So is Ugliness

It was some time before the noise of the doorbell penetrated Ian's drum roll. I let Mum answer the door, after all, she was already on her feet and I was still resting on the sofa. I recognised the voices of our nearest neighbours, nos 9 and 13.

'Mrs Stirling, what's going on in here?' I heard Mr no 9 asking. 'It sounds as if you've got a pile driver upstairs.'

'That's Ian. He's an oily rag,' Mum sighed.

'Just because he goes to that cathedral school doesn't make him more holy than the rest of us!' snapped the woman from no 13.

'Not "holy", I said "oily"–' began Mum but Mr no 9 wouldn't let her get any further.

'–and who keeps thumping on the bathroom door? It's interfering with our TV reception.'

'Not Helen, definitely,' Mum answered.

I sighed. It looked as if my exceptional diplomatic skills were needed. I joined Mum at the door. Mrs no 13 was off, 'That drumming goes right through you,' she explained, 'like... like–'

'–a dose of salts?' I suggested, giving her a friendly smile.

She shook her head, '–like a knife. It goes through you like a knife.'

Piercing. Knives don't go through you, and if they did you'd have more than a headache, but, tactful as ever, I didn't point this out. And the charm offensive paid off because Mrs no 13 smiled at me and said, 'David? My, you *have* grown.'

I'd grown from four foot eight to five foot seven inches in less than a year so I had heard this comment before. Strangely enough, I'd also noticed for myself, but I just grinned back and was beginning to think that the mood of the mob was changing when no 13's husband chipped in.

'Yes,' he said, 'that's why the stairs reverberate. It's him leaping about.'

I stood still, trying to look like someone who rarely moved.

I can get up the stairs in three steps and reach the top before the sitting-room door slams, but I decided not to mention this and no 13 got the conversation back to the subject of the drumming. 'That's what brings on the migraine,' she said. 'They last about three days, after which I go completely deaf – and numb. No feeling in my ears at all ...'

A red BMW pulled up outside.

'... then paralysis spreads down one side. First the right side, though you can still feel a tingling in your fingers ...'

A middle-aged man in a sharp suit got out and stared at the house. I hoped he might be a distraction, but the doorstep crowd was unstoppable.

'This can't all be due to Ian's drumming, surely,' Mum exclaimed.

'Quite right, Mrs Stirling. Quite right,' said Mrs no 13. 'There's also the thumping on the bathroom walls. Last Wednesday we couldn't watch telly because our wall started to judder. What was going on?'

'May I interrupt?' came a new voice from the back. It was the man from the BMW.

But no 9 got in first. 'Now, look, Mrs Stirling,' he said, using his I'm-a-reasonable-man type of voice. 'I'm a reasonable man, but the noise has got to stop. It's affecting my wife's nerves.'

Mum said in a small voice, 'I am sorry. We'll all make a determined effort to keep the noise down.'

At that moment the hat stand in the hall corner that I was leaning against toppled over. As coats and hats fell around me, I made a grab for some of them and discovered I was holding on to the tracksuit top I'd lost three months before.

'Great!' I shouted. I looked up to find a circle of grim-faced neighbours glaring at me.

The stranger looked even more care-worn than they did, though he attempted a smile. 'I just wanted to say–' he began.

'Let me finish this first!' snapped Mr no 9.

'Here,' he said, handing Mum an envelope, 'this is for you.'

Mum reached forward to take the envelope reluctantly, and I closed the door quickly. The chimes went again immediately.

'Don't open it,' I said firmly.

I could see Mum was worried about the letter. The neighbours had shaken her. I took the brown envelope from her. There was no number on it, just:

Mrs C Stirling
Elm Close
Blackrock

'I'll open it for you, Mum,' I told her. I was beginning to fear the worst. Nos 9 and 13 could have ganged up to take legal action against us.

'What is it?' Mum asked, her voice shaking.

'I'm not sure. It's from Higgins & Stop, Solicitors.'

CHAPTER FOUR

The Letter

I followed Mum into the kitchen. She was turning the letter over in her hands, but not reading it. Dad, like Silver the cat, has an uncanny knack of knowing when to appear and when to disappear. He had missed the visit from the neighbours, now he came in followed by the man with the red BMW.

'I met this ...' Dad started. But when he saw Mum's face he left the man in the hall, closed the kitchen door and asked abruptly, 'What's up?'

'No 9 just gave me a solicitor's letter,' Mum told him.

Dad took the letter from me and read it through swiftly.

'Are they suing us?' Mum asked.

'Suing? Who?' Dad replied.

'The neighbours.'

Dad looked baffled. 'Why should they? They didn't know your uncle Albert, did they?'

It was Mum's turn to look baffled. 'Uncle Albert wouldn't complain about the noise we make. He lives hundreds of miles away in Waltham Abbey. Anyway he's tone deaf.'

Her face brightened for a moment. 'He wouldn't mind Ian being an Oily Rag. He'd be a wonderful neighbour!'

Dad was re-reading the letter from Higgins & Stop. 'Uncle Albert live next door? It's a bit late for that, I'm afraid,' he said, handing Mum the letter to read.

'Why?' I asked.

'He's dead.'

'And he's left his entire estate to me,' Mum said slowly, looking at the letter again as if she didn't quite believe it.

I'd only met my great uncle Albert a few times. He lived in Essex in the south of England, too far away for a day visit. And we never stayed overnight with him, Mum said it was too unhygenic. Great Uncle Albert was a miser. He kept deep within his house, surrounded by the junk that was stacked high all around him. Narrow corridors wound between the piles of newspapers, overflowing boxes and souvenirs from his travels. He had some brilliant things too. My favourite was a sailing ship woven out of glass. About a metre high, it stood on the mantelpiece in the sitting-room, covered by a glass dome. The sea was also glass, spun like white candy floss. Pirates – Long John Silver; sailors – Admiral Lord Nelson; all the swash-buckling films ever watched were compressed into that ship in my imagination.

'It's a death trap, that place,' Dad said once after we visited. 'One dropped match and that lot'd go up like a bonfire.'

'It's too damp for that,' Mum snorted. 'Did you see the mould on the walls?'

Great Uncle Albert looked like a city gent who'd fallen into a pile of coal dust and carried on without stopping to wash himself. The suit he wore was constantly thick, dark and shiny.

'Great Uncle Albert's very old and frail,' Mum always said, but this made him sound weak and to me he was the opposite – fascinatingly different – a true eccentric. He talked about his dead brothers and sisters as if they were still alive, and confused all our names. We hadn't visited him for years and, since he never wrote or phoned ('a waste of good money'), we didn't know he had died until the solicitor's letter arrived.

'"Estate" means everything he owned,' Dad was explaining.

'Dear old Albert,' said Mum affectionately.

'How old was he?' I asked.

Mum tried to calculate. 'Let's see. He was Granny's older brother. She was seventy-seven when she died and that was when you were still in a buggy, so that's ...'

She gave up. 'Oh, about ninety.'

'Not bad, considering he still rode his bicycle until last year,' said Dad admiringly.

'He used to say "I'm ready to go any time",' Mum recalled, looking weepy.

'The ones who say that always last the longest,' said Dad.

'But I never thought he'd leave me

everything – dear Albert!' said Mum.

'How much?' asked Ian, entering the kitchen. The drums had been silent for some time, he had obviously overheard the news.

'Thousands – when we've sold the house.'

I let out a whoop of delight, then picked Mum up and twirled her round. Ian was chanting, 'It could be you!'

Just then Helen entered the kitchen with the BMW driver trailing behind her. 'This is Harry,' she said.

'Nice to meet ya, Harry!' said Ian, slapping him on the back. Though he was a strange-looking bloke, we were in the mood to welcome anyone.

I put Mum down. 'What's going on?' asked Helen. 'Have we won the lottery?'

'As good as. Great Uncle Albert's dead!' Ian replied.

Very carefully, Harry said, 'Presumably he was not a favourite uncle.'

That changed the mood.

'Quite,' said Dad, casting a sheepish look at Mum. 'Wonderful old gentleman, Albert,' he said. 'Er, sorry, Barry.'

'Harry,' corrected Helen.

'Sorry, Harry. What must you think of us? May we offer you a cup of tea?'

Mum and Dad were moving into Formal Hospitality Mode, which was odd: they didn't usually do this for Helen's boyfriends, but then Helen's boyfriends weren't usually middle-aged men.

When Helen objected to Harry being given a mug and went in search of the best china, Ian and I escaped upstairs.

'Who's he to tell us how we should feel about Albert?' Ian asked resentfully. We'd both liked Great Uncle Albert. He'd never spoken to us in a special voice for children. He barked at us just as he barked at everyone else. He would whack me over the head with a rolled-up newspaper. I always recognised this as a sign of friendship. On one visit he gave me a Davy pit helmet – a real one that miners wore to go down into the coal pit. I wondered whether he'd been a coal miner but when I asked Mum she said he'd worked for the Co-op all his life.

I was sorry Great Uncle Albert was dead.

Alive he would never have moved to Elm Close, to Dublin, or anywhere else. In fact, he'd refused Mum's invitation to come and live with us, much to Dad's relief. Albert wouldn't have left those mysterious piles of belongings, but now he was separated from them forever.

'Miserable git,' I said, and I didn't mean Albert.

CHAPTER FIVE

Plans are Drawn Up

Ian came into the kitchen with another catalogue full of pictures of drum kits.

'Mum, take a look at this! It's the best on the market!'

Mum flung off her rubber gloves in exasperation. 'Ian, how many times do I have to explain this? We haven't any more money yet. We have to sell Uncle Albert's house first, and before we do that we'll have to clear out the contents. That will be a nightmare! Uncle Albert hasn't thrown anything out since war was declared in 1939.'

'Why was he like that?' I asked. 'Why did he hoard everything?'

Mum considered for a moment. 'Well, he was

brought up in the days of real poverty. He would have been lucky to share a pair of shoes with one of his brothers or sisters. People didn't have the number of possessions we take for granted nowadays. They kept things carefully. Albert never lost the habit.'

'Much better for the environment – a careful use of resources,' said Helen, who was measuring out a diet portion of muesli. This from a person who'd cut down the Rain Forests if it would result in a new shade of lipstick.

She opened a glossy magazine. 'Mum, can I have a Paul Costello suit? Harry says it's under-stated quality.'

'Harry says,' repeated Mum bitterly, then added, under her breath, 'How often must I hear those words?'

'Harry is a professional image consultant,' Helen reminded us. 'He should know.'

'Yes, dear,' replied Mum, unconvinced. 'Now, back to the real world, who wants to help with stage one: clearing out Uncle Albert's house?'

'It's a long way,' objected Ian.

Mum nodded. 'It'll take three days. One day to get there, one to do the clearing out, and a day to travel back.'

'Can't,' said Helen emphatically. I've got a special date–'

'–with the suit!' I finished for her.

'I haven't even decided when we're going yet,' Mum pointed out.

'Well, I'm bound to be busy. We're doing electrolysis next week,' said Helen.

'What's that?' I asked. It sounded like electrocution.

'Pulling hairs off people,' Mum explained.

'Have you been practising on Harry?' I asked. He was nearly bald, though the bit of hair that did grow was pulled back into a ponytail.

'Can we fly over?' interrupted Ian. I could tell he was searching for a way out too.

'No, of course we can't,' Dad chipped in. 'We'll probably want to bring lots of things back with us, so it's got to be the ferry.'

'So you're going too, Dad?' Helen asked hopefully.

'Yes,' Dad answered. 'I'm going to contact

the estate agents and put the house on the market.'

'I'd definitely help if it was just a day but the pressure's really building up for the Leaving Cert,' whined Ian.

Mum and Dad looked impressed. Study was usually the last thing Ian worried about. But they missed the look he and Helen had given each other. As kids when Helen and Ian were forced to let me join in their games, that was the look they gave each other after they'd found a way of leaving me behind. Once, when I was six, they left me in the cupboard under the stairs for hours under the impression that we were playing 'Hide and Seek'.

I guessed that they wanted the house free of Mum, Dad or me. To test my suspicion, I said, 'Yeah, I'll help.'

I was right, Ian and Helen beamed at each other.

'Good lad!' Dad said, stretching over the breakfast clutter to pat me on the back.

'Wonderful!' Mum agreed. They were over-doing the praise a bit to annoy Ian and Helen.

'Yeah, wonderful!' drawled Ian. 'Brute strength's what's needed for this job. Let's face it, if brains were potatoes, David wouldn't have enough for a bag of chips!'

I heard Helen giggling at this as they left the room together.

Mum planned the trip to Waltham Abbey like an SAS Officer on a mission. Soon she'd fixed the dates (a week ahead in my mid-term break), booked the ferry to and from Holyhead and begun planning what we should take with us.

My list included: walkman, packets of biscuits, cans of Coke, bars of chocolate and a copy of *Great Moments in Rugby*. Mum's included vacuum cleaner, step ladder and black refuse bags. All Dad could think of was sleeping bags.

'Sleeping bags? What's wrong with the beds?' I asked.

An unfortunate question. Mum started to describe the beds in Great Uncle Albert's terraced house. Dust mites, bed bugs, creeping dermatitis. All in all, sleeping in one of those old beds seemed to be a slow way of committing suicide.

'Why don't we stay in a hotel?' I asked.

'Take too long, cost too much,' Dad explained. 'Don't worry,' he assured me, 'we'll go out for meals, but we'll just camp down on the floor.'

'In the sitting-room?'

'If you like.'

'Okay.' The sailing ship would be in view. I'd be in my sleeping bag and be able to imagine the sailors in their hammocks.

At least I'd get good food – no weevils in ship's biscuits for me.

CHAPTER SIX

The Journey

A week later, we were on our way. As we slowed down outside Birmingham Mum and Dad got nostalgic.

'Look at this traffic!' exclaimed Dad. 'Do you remember when it took us only six hours to reach Uncle Albert's house?'

'When Helen and Ian were little! When Ian was still in a car-seat,' reminisced Mum.

They launched into the cute things Helen and Ian had done and said when they were young. 'Ian's first word was tractor,' Mum recalled. 'Only he used to say "twactor". Remember?'

Dad repeated 'twactor' and chuckled.

'We'd spend the whole journey counting twactors,' Mum laughed.

Sad, isn't it? One thing you can be sure about everyone is that they've been young in the past, so why parents get so worked up about it is a mystery. These conversations about 'the good old days' made me uneasy. They showed how Mum and Dad yearned for a simpler time when their kids were little and easy to control. Little kids: little problems; big kids: big problems.

'I bet Ian isn't counting *twactors* now!' I said grimly. I had a rough idea what he might be doing. I'd seen him heaving a crate of stout up the stairs the evening before we'd left. More mysteriously, Helen was browsing through cookery books. But I said nothing. I didn't want Dad to turn the car round. I wanted to see Great Uncle Albert's house again.

The traffic crawled through Waltham Cross, but I didn't mind. I liked looking at the stone cross that stands in the middle of the junction. Dad told me the cross was built on the orders of an English king. It marked the place where the coffin of his dead wife had rested overnight on the journey south to bury her. That was centuries ago. But here was the cross, still jamming up the traffic – except now the jam was caused by cars – machines that the king couldn't have imagined. But he'd found a way to make sure his wife wasn't forgotten. Great Uncle Albert had lived and died just a few miles away, but who knew or cared? Who would remember him in a hundred years time?

I resolved to find something of Great Uncle Albert's to keep. 'You shouldn't live and die forgotten,' I said to myself, then realised, as Mum and Dad looked back at me with surprise, that I'd spoken aloud.

CHAPTER SEVEN

The Ship

The car drew up outside Great Uncle Albert's house. Dad deposited Mum and myself on the pavement and drove off to explore the estate agents and restaurants.

We stood outside the house, and Mum sighed. 'I remember coming here as a child ... This'll be the last time.'

Small though the houses were, they looked out on a river which gave an almost rural impression to the surroundings. It looked like 'Coronation Street' with a bit more grass and water.

'Cliff Richard used to live in this road,' Mum told me.

'Who?'

'Cliff Richard! You know, "We're All Going on a Summer Holiday".' She actually began to sing!

'Yes, yes, I know,' I said hastily, looking around to make sure that no-one had heard.

'He was very kind to the old people,' Mum went on. 'And the Shadows lived around here too. I once went to a wedding where they were guests.'

'Great,' I said, dismissively. If nostalgia was a hereditary condition then I was in big trouble. I headed towards the house. 'Where do we start?'

Mum pulled herself together.

'Ruthlessness is the key,' she told me. 'If in doubt, throw it out. Look!' A large yellow skip stood in Great Uncle Albert's front garden. In fact, it nearly filled the whole plot.

'I've booked that for two days,' said Mum. 'I expect to fill it.'

I nodded. I was beginning to realise that this was more a mission of destruction than exploration.

Mum pulled out the bulky keys that Higgins & Stop had sent her and placed a key in the lock. She pushed and pulled on the door. The lock was effective but the door looked as if it would come off its hinges at the slightest shove.

Mum turned to me, 'It's difficult to believe Uncle Albert isn't here to let us in.' That was all that it took for me to visualise him in the hallway, heading towards the door. He had an eccentric way of saying hello. The front door would open but he'd already be disappearing into the kitchen. 'Kettle's on,' he'd say over his shoulder. That was the greeting we'd get for travelling across the Irish Sea and two hundred miles to see him. How he knew it was us at the door I never understood. Perhaps he peered out of the window first, or maybe he had so few visitors that he knew it wasn't anyone else. Perhaps everyone got the kettle's-on treatment.

When the door creaked opened and we entered the narrow hallway I sensed that Mum wished for that greeting too.

The same musty smell, the same brown wallpaper, heaps of belongings, but no Uncle Albert.

I went into what he had called the 'scullery'. There was his stove and the famous kettle, dull grey and cold.

Mum had followed me in and was staring

around at the familiar objects.

'Let's have a look around before we start,' I suggested.

Mum didn't reply so I wandered into the sitting-room. There, still, were the bundles of newspapers tied with string, and the familiar furniture – every surface covered with objects to stock a Car Boot sale.

My eyes turned to the mantelpiece. Still there! – the sailing ship made of thousands of strands of delicate glass, woven into shape in clear red, white and blue. When I had first seen it, the ship was bigger than me, and I'd stared up at it on the giant mantelpiece. Ever since, I'd missed no opportunity to steal into the room and gaze at it, until at last I was tall enough to examine it at eye level. Now I could touch it.

There were tiny glass sailors climbing up the ship's rigging. Their uniforms were moulded perfectly, even to the detail of navy ribbons round their caps.

Pushing my way through the stacks of magazines that were piled in front of the fireplace, I reached over and tried to lift the ship down. It wouldn't move. 'It's stuck!'

Mum came in. 'Yes, he often did that.'

'You mean he glued things down?'

'Yes, so no-one could steal them.'

I gripped the dome and lifted it off. It was covered in dust, like everything else in the house. But inside, the intricate glass ship was perfectly clean, the glass was so fine it was like lace, yet it was a real sailing ship to me. All my life I'd pictured it buffeted by winds on the high seas in the time of pirates and buccaneers. Mum thought it was something to do with the Crystal Palace Exhibition. Now I'd never be able to ask Great Uncle Albert about it. Like most of our family history on Mum's side, the English side, it was lost ...

Then my dream turned into a nightmare. Perhaps I knocked the ship when I removed the dome, but as I looked at the glass ship, it began to crumble. First the rigging collapsed, then the sails. One after another the fine strands fell until there was no more than a pile of red, white and blue glass chips.

I gasped in horror.

Mum looked up from the pile of newspapers she was inspecting. 'Okay?' she asked.

What could I say? A dream had fallen to pieces before my eyes.

'The ship,' I said inadequately

'David! How did you do that?'

'It just happened.'

Mum groaned. 'You must be more careful,' she said, because she always said that if I was within a hundred metres of something that broke, not because she cared about the ship.

'It was old age,' I said. 'It just crumbled.'

Mum sighed. 'It happens to people too. Clear up the bits.'

I swept up the pieces and threw them on the skip.

Dad returned an hour or so later. Most of the estate agents were shut, so he was going to have to try again the next day. Clearing out was going to be left to Mum and me.

Dad had found somewhere to eat though. There was a steak restaurant just a mile away.

When we returned to the house having eaten, we were so tired that we just took our sleeping bags, cleared spaces on the floor and slept.

No ghost of Uncle Albert kept us awake. Wherever he was he wasn't in the house, but I went to sleep wondering if dead people weren't just the sum of their possessions.

CHAPTER EIGHT

The Medal

There was no bathroom in the house. The loo was built on to the outside of the scullery. The cistern was still filling noisily and I was heading back to the scullery, when I heard a voice.

'You'll be Fred.' An artful, wizened face was showing over the back fence. 'You'll be Fred,' its voice said again. Was this an identification or a prediction?

'Sorry, no,' I answered.

'Not Maud's youngest?'

Thanks to the way Great Uncle Albert had confused our family, I was ready for this. 'No, I'm Albert's sister's daughter's youngest.'

'Albert didn't have a daughter.'

'No, Albert's sister's daughter's ...' I gave up. The old fellow was either eight feet tall or he was having to stand on something to look over the fence. 'I'm David,' I said.

The head disappeared, and, three feet shorter, its owner arrived at the beach gate. 'I'm Cyril Bently. I've been Albert's neighbour for fifty years.'

He opened the gate and edged me towards the back door.

Mum and Dad weren't keen on visitors, but Cyril Bently sat down at the table in the back parlour and seemed set to stay.

That was enough to get Dad moving. He took me out to a nearby café for breakfast, but when we returned old Cyril was still seated at the table, newly piled high with Great Uncle Albert's possessions.

'Mr Bently's been telling me how he won a medal,' said Mum, 'and I've given him a few little things to remember Uncle Albert by.' Four cushions, a big clock, a copy of Constable's 'Haywain' and three pairs of boots.

'We often had tea together,' said the old man, eyeing the huge brown teapot.

'Would you like the teapot, as a memento?'

said Mum, reverently.

'What medal?' I asked.

'I will take the teapot. Those cups match it, I think.' Mr Bently nodded and pointed.

'What medal did you win?' I asked again.

'Would you like the cups too?' Mum asked. 'David, don't delay Mr Bently any longer,' she said, fixing me with a look.

'No,' Dad agreed. He tried to pile the cushions, clock and boots into the old man's outstretched hands, but it was obvious he couldn't handle the lot.

I grabbed them. 'I'll help Mr Bently with these,' I said as he shuffled reluctantly towards the door.

'Make sure you come back immediately,' Dad said loudly, then, more softly, he added, 'alone.'

Mr Bently and I moved at a snail's pace along the road.

'What medal did you win, Mr Bently?' I asked.

But his only answer was: 'He probably had teaspoons to go with those cups.'

I couldn't get another word out of him until I

dumped the things in his hallway. Then he said, 'Silver ones, I'll be bound,' and shut the door in my face.

When I arrived back, Dad was hurrying away to the estate agents. His haste was explained as soon as I got inside. Another elderly neighbour was sitting at the oak table.

'This is Mrs Ridgewell,' Mum said. It was scarcely an introduction as Mrs Ridgewell was in full flow.

'So, Cyril Bently's managed it after all those years,' she was saying bitterly, but with a hint of admiration. 'Albert wouldn't have him under his roof while he was alive and now he's got his hands on half his belongings.'

'So they weren't lifelong friends?' Mum asked weakly.

'Lifelong enemies more like.'

'Did Mr Bently really win a medal?' I asked.

'Spent most of the war down an air-raid shelter,' answered Mrs Ridgewell contemptuously. 'And not always alone, if you take my meaning,' she said, nodding at Mum.

'Yes, well, it would be wonderful to listen to

you all day,' said Mum hastily, 'but we must get on.' She almost took the chair from under Mrs Ridgewell.

The old lady kept up her commentary as she walked down the hall. 'Not a decent bone in his body,' she said. Then, turning at the door, she added, 'No, it was Albert who won the medal.'

The door closed on her. Mum said fiercely. 'David, not another word about medals! I want you working now.'

❋ ❋ ❋

I decided on my strategy. I would grab a load of something bulky, like clothes, throw them into the skip, then I would have time to take a look round. I headed first for Great Uncle Albert's bedroom. I scooped out the contents of the rickety old wardrobe and staggered out to the skip with them.

Then I opened a drawer in a heavy mahogany chest. A muddle of socks, none of them in pairs, faced me. None of them even matched. I tried to imagine Great Uncle Albert wearing un-matching socks, hidden beneath his dark suit.

Yes, more than possible.

I heaped the socks into a black plastic sack and opened the next drawer. Underwear. I emptied the contents without looking at them, then opened a third drawer. There was a tangle of unironed shirts with their arms locked together as if they were fighting. I pulled two apart. They were made of some thick, warm material. They had no collars, just little white buttons where collars could be attached. Before his Oily Rag days, Ian would have liked them. But not now, so I stuffed them into the sack, dragged them all to the skip and emptied them out. As I came back into the house, I found Mum with her head deep inside a sideboard.

'Found anything?' I asked.

Her voice came out muffled from the sideboard. 'Anything!' she gasped, emerging. 'What have you in mind? Twenty-year-old bars of soap? Pre-war digestive biscuits? I've found them all.'

'Anything *interesting*,' I emphasised. I liked the sound of the biscuits, but I knew Mum well enough to know they'd be in the skip by now.

She was getting exasperated by the heaps of stuff. 'I'm not going to sort through it anymore,' she told me. 'I'm just going to scoop it into bags.'

I nodded. If I could just watch as she shovelled things in, like on a conveyor belt, then I could pick out anything of interest, like a medal.

'Did you know Great Uncle Albert had won a medal?' I asked.

'Well, Mr Bently's story did sound familiar,' she said in a distracted sort of way.

'What medal was it?'

'The George Cross.'

'When did he win it?' I asked her.

She frowned. 'In World War Two.'

'Well, I know that!' This was hopeless. 'I didn't think they handed them out at the Co-op Bakery,' I answered, hoping to prod Mum into remembering something. 'But what did he win it *for*?' I persisted.

This time her voice came from deep inside a cupboard. 'Er, bravery, I think.' And this was the person who disapproved when my Maths report said I should pay more attention to detail.

'Poor Great Uncle Albert!' I said. 'Fancy winning a medal and your family just ignoring it. I bet he died of a broken heart.'

'Well, he took long enough about it. He lived another fifty years,' came the cupboard voice.

'Fifty years after what?' I asked. 'Where was he fighting? Was he an officer? Surely you must remember something.'

Mum reappeared from the cupboard. 'David, I'm up to my ears in the accumulated dirt and grime of half a century here. As far as I'm concerned, I'm the one who deserves a medal. Now go and get on with something useful.'

'Just one more question,'

'Just one.'

'Did Great Uncle Albert mention the medal in his will? Did he leave it to anyone in particular?'

Mum shook her head. 'No.' Then she added, 'But you can have it if you find it, so long as you get on with some work.'

I was delighted. I would shift every item in the house if it meant I could have Great Uncle Albert's medal.

CHAPTER NINE

The Search

I started immediately. I searched every drawer and cupboard in Great Uncle Albert's house, including the pantry cupboards. The medal was in none of them.

'Perhaps he lost it,' Mum suggested. 'Or gave it away.'

But I knew he wouldn't have done either.

Mum grew more irritated. 'David, we've just one day to clear this whole house. You're making it more untidy, if that's possible. I *insist* you clear out the rubbish instead of chucking it from one place to another.'

Dutifully, I spent the next couple of hours loading stuff on the skip. By the time I was finished, it was nearly full.

That evening Mum stood in the empty sitting-room. Its emptiness pleased her, but to me it meant there was little chance of finding the medal.

'If I called round to visit Mrs Ridgewell, I could ask her about the medal,' I suggested.

'No more elderly neighbours!' cried Mum. 'Come on, give me a hand with this old chair,' she instructed, taking hold of the last piece of furniture in the room.

Reluctantly I grabbed hold. 'It weighs a ton,' I complained, as we lugged it towards the front door.

'Uncle Albert probably stuffed it full of five-pound notes,' joked Mum.

I dropped my side of the chair. 'Of course.'

'David, I was only joking,' Mum protested.

'I know, but that's exactly the sort of thing he would do,' I jabbered. 'Put something valuable in a good hiding place!'

I was too excited to speak clearly. Suddenly I was sure I knew where the medal was.

I raced out to the skip, delighted with my idea. Then I saw the state of the skip. A mountain of furniture, old rugs and junk of all sorts sat there. And I knew the socks were right at the bottom.

I clambered onto the pile.

'None of that rubbish is coming in here again!' yelled a voice from an open upstairs window.

'I only need one sock,' I called back. One after another I threw objects off the skip.

It took twenty minutes before I glimpsed the dark mess of socks nestling at the bottom. I dragged an old burnt pot and grey mattress off the pile, desperate to reach them.

The upstairs window opened again and Mum poked her head out. She looked as if she was about to be guillotined, and she had an expression to match. 'Every item is going back in that skip, David, even if you don't find what you're looking for.'

'Promise,' I called out recklessly. I had reached the socks. I grabbed one and plunged my hand in. Nothing. I tried another.

Mum's curiosity got the better of her. 'Found anything?' she asked, still from the upstairs window.

But I was silent, amazed at what I had discovered wedged into the toe of one sock.

'David! What's the matter? Are you okay?'

I gulped. A ten-pound note. Another sock rustled as I felt it. 'The socks are filled with money!' I cried.

Within seconds Mum was downstairs and clambering on to the skip, using the chairs that I had chucked out. Together we searched for socks. Each contained a single ten-pound note.

'Twelve, thirteen,' Mum was counting excitedly. 'That's one hundred and thirty pounds.'

I pointed to a tangle of shirts. 'We might have missed some. Let's look in that lot.'

'Aha!' cried Mum, after plunging her hand amongst the shirts. 'What's this?' She unearthed a small pile of socks. I never thought the sight of Great Uncle Albert's old socks would fill me with such excitement. Each rustling sock delivered another ten-pound note.

'One hundred and sixty,' I whistled. 'Wonderful socks.'

'How did you guess?' asked Mum.

'I didn't,' I confessed. 'I wasn't looking for money.'

'What were you looking for then?'

'For his medal.' I tried to explain what it meant to me. It was connected to my disappointment about the glass ship. 'I wanted something of Great Uncle Albert's ...'

Mum nodded as if she understood. 'Well, how about this?' she asked brightly, pointing to a plaster statue lying on the lawn. It was a shepherd boy about three feet high. Age had faded all the colours to a murky green and the nose was broken off.

'I threw it away when I was cleaning out the sitting-room. I didn't know you wanted to keep something,' said Mum apologetically.

'Well, not just anything ...' The tall boy was no great work of art.

'Remember how Uncle Albert used to keep his trilby hat on it?' Mum reminded me. 'It always stood on the sideboard.'

Great Uncle Albert was an incredible shot. He would take off his hat and spin it at the tall boy from the sitting-room door. He never missed.

'Yes,' I said. 'I'll take it.'

'Good,' said Mum. 'So now you have two

things to remember your great uncle by. The tall boy and the money.'

I was puzzled. 'The money?'

'Yes,' said Mum. 'You found it, David. It's yours.'

✿ ✿ ✿

As we drove away the next morning, my final view was of Cyril Bently clambering onto the skip in search of more mementos of his non-existent friendship with my great uncle Albert.

CHAPTER TEN

The Party's Over

The first sign of trouble back at Elm Close was the net curtains billowing out of open windows.

'It's far too cold to have all those windows open,' said Mum. 'So much for our nice warm house.'

Dad was silent. He pulled into the drive, leapt out and headed towards the front door.

Mum stood on the front lawn pointing. 'What's that?' she asked indignantly. A sprinkling of cans littered the grass.

'Some passer-by must've ...' I began, although I already recognised the brand that Ian had been sneaking into the house before we left.

Dad's shout from inside interrupted, 'Come and look at this.'

I charged in ahead of Mum. Compared to this

the ferry from Holyhead looked neat and tidy. Cans and crisp packets clung to every surface except the ceiling. Most of the furniture was shoved back in one corner. Mum rushed towards the television set. 'Blood!' she shrieked.

I scratched the dry red stain on the screen. 'Lipstick,' I corrected. 'Someone's written ...' I traced the letters and shut up.

'What does it say?' asked Mum, as I tried to rub out the words with the sleeve of my jumper. At least I managed to smear them so that they were illegible.

'Exam pressure,' shouted Dad. 'I'll give Ian exam pressure. This is what they had in mind.' He was pacing back and forth in the sitting-room. 'A party, the mother of all parties! Where are they?'

Mum suddenly looked worried. 'Perhaps it was intruders who did this, and they've harmed Helen and Ian.'

'Nonsense. Helen and Ian perpetrated this deed,' shouted Dad, looking as if he was ready to harm them himself.

'Then where are they?' wailed Mum.

'Not up yet, probably,' I said. I could see what the next few hours would be like. Any hope of a decent meal was gone. The sooner we started, the sooner the arguments would be over and I'd get fed.

I leapt up the stairs and into Helen's room, but it was empty and so was Ian's.

'They're not in their beds!' I shouted down. Downstairs I could hear windows being shut and Mum giving a commentary on the further damage she was finding.

I sat on the top stair and called down, 'They're not here!' If I managed to get Mum and Dad worried about Helen and Ian, they'd be easier on them when they did come face to face. Then this little crisis might be over in a decade or two ...

But Helen spoiled it all by coming out of the bathroom.

'David,' she said in a feeble voice, 'I have a headache.' She was wearing a long silky dressing-gown and gliding about like Greta Garbo in one of those old black-and-white films, while I had just endured a lousy ferry journey and was close to death by starvation. As usual there was no gratitude for my help.

'No kidding!' I said more loudly. I resented her manner. 'Helen's up here,' I called down the stairs, 'And she's got a *headache*.'

The noises downstairs had changed pitch. I heard Ian's voice low and sulky, answering a battery of questions. I slid down a few stairs so I could observe what was happening. Ian was standing in the hall, looking decidedly rough. He was unshaven and beneath the stubble his skin was pale and blotchy. He clearly didn't like the questions, but one followed another so quickly he couldn't have answered even if he'd wanted to.

Eventually he exploded. 'Look!' he said so loudly that Mum and Dad stopped. Actually he meant 'listen' not 'look' but I didn't point that out – the atmosphere was tense.

In a monotone, as if he was explaining something of great simplicity to idiots, he said, 'I thought I'd have a few friends round. More than I expected turned up. Things got a bit … out of hand. I was airing the place and would have finished tidying up if Helen had helped.'

I admired the way he put it: 'finished', as if he had done hours of work and just needed a few more minutes to make the place perfect.

Helen heard her name and shot on to the landing. 'If I'd helped!' she shrieked. 'Why should I help clear up after your friends? They are some of the rudest, ugliest, most disgusting ... They completely ruined the gourmet dinner I cooked for Harry.'

'That was ruined the minute you turned on the oven,' said Ian wearily.

'So, in other words,' shouted Dad, 'you abused our trust. You ...' he jabbed a finger at Ian, 'did no work. And you ...' he turned to Helen, 'you devoted your time to trying to impress that pompous–'

'Harry is not pompous,' contradicted Helen. 'He's sophisticated. None of you know what that means.' She sank down on the stairs, sounding close to tears. 'You've never given Harry a chance ...'

'A chance to do what?' demanded Dad, but

more gently. He couldn't bear to see Helen cry, as she knew.

'I think I'll have hysterics,' complained Ian. 'She only has to sob into her hankie and Mum and Dad'll forgive anything.'

❀ ❀ ❀

But Mum and Dad had neither forgiven nor forgotten. We had to wait a few days to discover their plans, but the conspiratorial mutterings told us something was going on.

'What do you think they're up to?' Helen asked me nervously.

We had to wait until Friday evening to find out, when Dad declared he had an announcement to make. We filed into the sitting-room, trying to look unconcerned.

I picked up the latest *Radio Times*. 'David, put that down,' Mum ordered. I put it down, picked up the TV controls and turned the Eurosport channel on.

'David, will you turn that off. We have something very important to tell you,' insisted Mum.

'Are we going to have new curtains in the

sitting-room?' I asked. I could have watched TV with the sound turned down. The only drama I liked came on Eurosport.

'We are not doing anything,' snapped Mum. 'We are separating.'

Now this was a shock. We stayed quiet for a minute, then Helen, screwing up her lips in disapproval, said, 'You mean, you and Dad are splitting up?'

'No, no,' Dad tutted. 'We're not separating from each other. We're separating from you.' He waved a hand towards us as if flicking away insects.

'You can't–' I started to say, but my protests were drowned by the stupid, squealing noises Helen was making.

Ian seemed equally delighted. He came close to smiling. 'Great. We can have a place of our own,' he said.

'Next door to *us*,' Mum stressed. 'We'll hear everything you do.'

'But at a distance,' Dad added, beaming.

'We'll be the neighbours you have to consider,' Mum went on.

Helen stopped squealing and began to ask questions. 'So, we'll have two houses?'

'Two houses,' Dad confirmed. Ian thundered up the stairs and began a triumphant drum roll that reverberated throughout the house.

'Two of everything,' exclaimed Helen. 'Two bathrooms, two front doors, two TVs.'

'Two kitchens, two washing machines,' Mum added, in an attempt to bring Helen down to earth.

'Two telephones?' questioned Helen, ignoring her. 'Two telephones!' she sang in time to Ian's drumming as Mum nodded. 'Everything we want for ourselves.'

'Yes, but who's *we?*' I muttered. Mum and Dad had thought of an unusual way to stop family arguments. Helen and Ian would be close at hand but out of the firing line. They were all delighted. But nobody had mentioned me. Where was I to live?

CHAPTER ELEVEN

Farewell, Elm Close!

I tried to bring up the neglected subject of where I fitted into the new semi-detached Stirling family, but hardly had Mum and Dad made their announcement, than Dad delivered another piece of bad news.

'Before we leave Elm Close, we're going to give a party, a civilised party.'

'To show you three how to behave properly,' added Mum.

We'd wondered how they'd get their revenge, this was it.

Nos 9 and 13 were invited and the people across the street were warned the party was to take place. 'This is how to be considerate to one's neighbours,' explained Mum.

'What've they got to be warned about? You're only inviting the neighbours and four of Dad's colleagues from work. What are they going to do – start arguing loudly about Data Protection?' asked Ian.

'I hope not,' said Helen, prissily. 'I'm going to invite Harry.'

More bad news.

'So you're serious about him then?' asked Mum, unenthusiastically.

'How could she be anything else? That guy has no sense of humour,' complained Ian.

'Just because he doesn't behave in a childish manner,' snapped Helen.

'I've met geriatrics who're more fun,' said Ian.

Obviously, it was going to be a wonderful party ...

❀ ❀ ❀

When our next-door neighbours realised it was a farewell party, they accepted enthusiastically. Helen was disappointed: she dreaded them talking to Harry.

'Do they have to come?' she asked. 'They've

always hated us.'

'They'll realise how they've misjudged us,' Mum said, contradicting herself by adding: 'I've a good mind to sell the house to the nastiest person I can find.'

'Harry?' suggested Ian.

'Harry will be able to chat with my colleagues,' said Dad.

'Put him next to someone interesting and very, very respectable,' pleaded Helen.

'Invite Mother Teresa,' I suggested.

'Is she a good conversationalist?' asked Helen.

She must have had her sense of humour surgically removed since meeting Harry.

The punitive party was in what Mum and Dad inaccurately called 'full swing'. I was handing out cheesy nibbles and Ian, a tortured expression on his face, was playing Richard Clayderman favourites on the piano. The doorbell rang.

The conversation about protecting data was just getting lively, when the two uniformed officers walked into the sitting-room.

'We can't be making too much noise, surely!' exclaimed Mum.

'This is about the incident the other night,' said one of the officers.

'Incident? What incident?'

Then the whole story came out. Some of Ian's uninvited Heavy Metal friends had arrived as Helen was serving Chicken Provençal to Harry at a candlelit supper.

Ian's pals started duelling with the lighted candlesticks on the pavement outside. When a bush caught on fire, the neighbours had called the Gardaí.

No wonder Ian and Helen weren't the best of friends.

I tried to console Harry. 'You were lucky. If you'd eaten Helen's cooking, you'd probably be dead by now.'

But Harry refused to be consoled, even when I pointed out that they weren't pressing charges.

'I'm not accustomed to being interviewed by the police,' he replied.

'One disaster after another,' complained Dad

when the bemused guests had left. 'The sooner we separate, the better!'

❋   ❋   ❋

But there was a lot of work to do before that happened.

'You've got no idea how much is involved in selling two houses and buying another two,' Dad lectured me. He'd taken a day off work to visit estate agents and was sitting at the kitchen table surrounded by house brochures. 'Agents appointed, prospective buyers shown around, contracts drawn up. It's a difficult business, I can tell you.' He made it sound like a full-time occupation.

'But at least we're better off,' I pointed out encouragingly. 'We must be. After all, Mum's inherited a house.'

But if there's one thing my Dad dislikes, it's being made to feel fortunate when he's dwelling on how hard done-by he is.

'Ah well, theoretically, that's true,' he admitted gloomily as he leafed through the details. 'But there's going to be an awful lot of extra expense in equipping two houses ...' He shoved some of the brochures to one side. 'We won't be able to afford those.'

He'd been unnerved by the way Helen was prancing about with glossy interiors magazines and talking about her house's decor.

'It's just going to be decorated. There'll be no decor,' Dad had said with emphasis.

'I'm looking for clean, fresh lines,' Helen continued, waving her arms about and totally ignoring him, 'with the best of modern design.' Obviously no expense was to be spared.

Ian regarded the move as his chance to launch the Oily Rags on to the serious Heavy Metal scene. He was ready with an ad: 'The Oily Rags Heavy Metal (Thrash) Band, available for gigs.' All he was waiting for was his new address and phone number to put the card in every Dublin music shop, so he was eager to house-hunt.

I trailed around with Dad and Ian while Mum concentrated on trying to sell the house in Waltham Abbey.

Ian's first question was always, 'What are the neighbours like?' He refused to consider houses on new developments just in case awkward people moved in next door. His definition of 'awkward' was anyone who disliked music.

'Surely we're not looking for two houses next door to an Oily Rags fan?' I objected. 'The chances must be millions to one.'

'I didn't know the Oily Rags had any fans,' said Dad.

'Then what are we looking for?' I asked. 'A saint?'

Eventually, we found just the neighbour we were looking for – not quite a saint, but the next best thing to it ...

'She's deaf,' Ian told us with delight after visiting the person living at no 6 Highfield Road. 'She's little and old and I had to yell at her to be heard.'

We'd already inspected nos 8 and 10 Highfield Road which were both for sale. Now Ian became wildly enthusiastic about buying them.

'Look how convenient this is to the city centre,' he pointed out as we stood on the pavement outside the red-brick terrace. 'They are both properties of character with many attractive features ...'

'You sound like that estate agent fellow,' re-marked Dad sourly. We'd learnt that estate agents used the English language in an entirely abnormal way. 'Interesting' meant 'odd' and 'great potential' meant 'uninhabitable'. Once, Dad was told that a house 'boasted a spacious garden', he peered over the fence and asked, 'Is the huge garden on the other side?'

'The living-rooms are surprisingly large,' urged Ian.

'Rather poky, I thought,' answered Dad. He felt he was only doing his duty if he thought of every possible objection to any property we looked at.

'Full central heating–'

'–that'll cost a bomb to run.'

'With the added attraction of open fireplaces in the living-rooms.'

'Have you any idea how much work is involved in laying a coal fire?' asked Dad indignantly.

'Both houses have fully modernised bath-rooms,' said Ian, changing tack, 'and tastefully refurbished kitchens.'

'–and, best of all, a neighbour who can't hear,' I

chipped in. 'The ideal listener to the Oily Rags.'

'Quite appalling the selfishness of Modern Youth,' grumbled Dad. 'Fancy revelling in the disability of a little old lady.'

He scowled at Ian and headed off down the alleyway to the side of no 10, looking up hopefully for signs that the roof was caving in.

It didn't seem likely that we'd be moving to Highfield Road. I would have liked to because one of my best friends, Abbas, a refugee from Sri Lanka, lived down the hill at no 82.

But Ian was optimistic. I hadn't seen him so pleased since he got a tune out of a tuba. 'We've found our new home ... homes,' he commented as soon as Dad was out of earshot.

'How do you make that out?' I asked. 'Dad hasn't said one good word about the houses yet.'

'Yes,' replied Ian, 'but behind the moaning there was a real note of enthusiasm. Couldn't you hear it?'

I shook my head, and, not for the first time, wondered what wave-length my brother was tuned into.

CHAPTER TWELVE

Moving

But Ian was right. Dad was keen to buy nos 8 and 10 Highfield Road. When he told Mum about the two houses he sounded as enthusiastic as Ian. In fact, he'd recognised all sorts of advantages that Ian hadn't thought of.

'They're both vacant already,' I heard him tell Mum, 'So we'll have no bother about moving dates. They're identical terraced houses–'

'Terraced?' Mum looked concerned. 'We don't want trouble with the neighbours.'

'But no 10 is end of terrace with an alleyway between it and no 12 and Mrs Denton-Mayhew at no 6 is – how's this for a bit of luck? – completely deaf.' And that from the man who complains about the selfishness of youth!

'Maybe we should try somewhere with no neighbours,' I suggested. 'We could move into the country, surrounded by fields and sheep.'

'No chance of that,' Dad replied dismissively. He had only one thing on his mind: he was intent on convincing Mum to buy nos 8 and 10 Highfield Road.

After one visit, Mum was persuaded. Mum and Dad had no difficulty selling Great Uncle Albert's house. They sold it at a knockdown bargain price, feeling apologetic about the state it was in – no inside bathroom, damp walls, peeling wallpaper – in fact, full of estate agent 'potential'. But knowing Great Uncle Albert's house was gone made him seem more distant, more dead than before. Though I hadn't forgotten the medal.

Soon nos 8 and 10 Highfield Road were ours. Mum and Dad spent all their spare time there, accompanied by Helen who insisted on supervising the work at no 8 herself. Ian was content to add his new address to the advertisement for the Oily Rags and wait for replies.

It was the last Saturday morning before we

moved. I'd spent the morning doing fierce battle on the rugby field and was lying on my bed, thinking about our 10:14 win, when Dad came in. He dumped a couple of tea chests and said, 'Get packing. We've got five days to move.'

I'd been waiting for this moment. 'Ah yes,' I said calmly, sitting up and fixing him with a look, 'Where to?'

He looked surprised. 'Highfield Road, David. Where else?'

I used the stare that TV lawyers use to intimidate a witness. 'I see. Highfield Road, which number, 8 or 10?' I asked.

'Helen and Ian to no 8. You, me and Mum to no 10, of course.'

I leapt up and circled the tea chests. 'Why am I going with you?'

'Because you're still only a child!'

A child! At twelve years of age. 'What do you mean? I'm bigger than any of you! Look.' I wanted to show him the exercise we do in rugby practice. I put my hands on his shoulders. 'Now stand still. Then fall backwards. Don't worry, I'll catch you.' I knew that I could handle the weight because flab is lighter than muscle.

But Dad got irritated. 'I haven't time for this nonsense. I've got to get on with the packing.'

'It'll only take a second. Keep your feet together and just fall back.'

'And end up with concussion? Stop being stupid, David.'

'Well, don't expect any help with the packing then,' I shouted as I thumped down the stairs.

It was great to think that, however much the neighbours complained now, it didn't matter.

CHAPTER THIRTEEN

David: 1
Parents: 0

There was no logic to Dad's attitude. Helen and Ian had behaved badly, yet I was the child who had to be watched.

I checked with Mum that she felt the same way. It's always worth asking the other parent if you get the wrong answer from the first, just in case they haven't conferred on what to say. But Mum was even more adamant than Dad that I should stay with them. Apparently if I wasn't there, she'd feel old.

'So I've got to live at no 10 just so you can feel young. And it won't work. You're getting older all the time,' I pointed out. It was obvious.

'Oh, Davy,' Mum said, starting to look dreamy-eyed, 'You're my little baby. I don't want to lose you yet.'

'Wouldn't it be a good idea if I left before you're sick of me? We could cut out the middle bit, all the arguing and just go straight to the separation.'

'David, Dad and I aren't "sick" of Helen and Ian. We just recognise that they're old enough to have a little more independence. You're not. What would people say if you didn't live with us?'

I hate that line of argument. What people? The neighbours again?

But I shut up. I'd have to work on Mum and Dad if I was going to move into no 8.

The advantages were obvious. My friends at school were in no doubt which house would be better.

'You'll have much more fun with your brother and sister,' advised Abbas. 'You know, her friends round, parties ...'

'And they can't tell you what to do,' said Joe. He had little sisters who were always getting in the way.

Helen and Ian wouldn't have rules about wiping your feet on the doormat and so on. In fact, the way Helen had decorated no 8, there wouldn't be anything as ordinary as a doormat.

I wasn't going to ask her for help. She wouldn't be keen to have me at no 8, but perhaps I could use that to my advantage. I started by reminding Mum and Dad of my last year's breakages: the dining-room table, which should have taken my weight, but hadn't; the lampstand; a telephone; doorknobs too numerous to list.

And I returned to my old habit of head-butting the light switches on and off.

'How's Psycho Phil?' I asked Ian as we sat down to supper one evening. 'Haven't seen him since he was thrown off the DART–'

But Helen interrupted. She was full of her plans for no 8. 'Colourwise, sharpness and vibrancy are in this year, Harry says.'

'Oh, does he?' said Dad, with a fair amount of sharpness and vibrancy himself. 'What's that to do with furnishing a house?'

'Dad, don't you know anything? Sharp colours are deep and clear. They have clarity and contrast. They're very nineties.'

'Harry says,' added Ian.

'Muted colours are out,' intoned Helen.

'I wish muted boyfriends were in,' complained Dad.

'Harry's paying a lot of attention to the decoration at no 8,' I observed to no one in particular. 'Anyone would think he was going to live there.'

'Over my dead body!' yelled Dad.

'Mine too,' agreed Ian.

I saw my chance. 'So, er, Ian, you wouldn't object if I lived at no 8?'

'No, that's fine with me.'

'All right, all right,' Dad cut in.

He looked across at Mum. But her mind was still on Harry. 'If he's so great, why is he still unmarried at his age?' she asked.

'*If* he's unmarried ...'

Dad cleared his throat and turned to Mum. 'David can live at no 8 if you agree.'

I thought Mum would resist but she nodded. 'It might encourage Helen and Ian to behave themselves,' she said.

She's such a dreamer, my mum.

Freedom

'This is great!'

Joe, Abbas and I sloped around no 8, Highfield Road inspecting the facilities. 'Cool.'

My friends were full of admiration. My bedroom didn't look very different from the way it was before with the same furniture from 11, Elm Close, apart from Great Uncle Albert's tall boy on the window sill. But the rest of the house was completely different.

'Ornaments are just clutter,' Helen told us all, as she gave the guided tour. 'And I'm aiming at clean, harmonious lines.'

Hypocritically, Joe and Abbas nodded in agreement, pretending that they knew what she was talking about. For some reason my friends seem to like my sister ... Actually, they spent more time looking at her than at the house which was like something from the next century.

Everything was either black or white. The carpets were thick white wool. The television, nearly as big as the screen at The Odeon, was black. Arranged round it were three black and white striped sofas – one for each of us, and littered around the room were large white bean bags. The old grand piano that Ian no longer used, reappeared at no 8 because it fitted in with the decor.

'You lucky so-and-so,' said Joe, throwing himself onto one of the sofas.

'Eight channels,' I said, flicking through them on the TV remote. I was enjoying myself.

I looked at the empty fireplace as my friends settled down to watch TV. We hadn't had an open fire at Elm Close, just central heating. I liked the thought of a blazing fire warming the room as we relaxed. Trouble was, we didn't have any coal.

'Pity we can't have a fire,' I said.

'Would it ruin the clean, harmonious lines?' asked Abbas. It's not always easy to tell when he's joking.

'No coal,' I answered.

He leapt up. 'I'll ask my Mum.'

'Anything to eat?' asked Joe hopefully after Abbas left. We drifted out to the kitchen in search of food. All the machines, including the fridge, were brand new and empty.

I slammed the fridge door shut, then brightened. 'The beauty of this system is that Mum is just next door!'

We found Mum enjoying herself unpacking tea chests. Her fridge was new too, but the plastic covering had gone and it was full of food. I took back some bread, peanut butter, biscuits and crisps.

Abbas was trying to light the fire by the time I got back. His Mum had given him a carrier-bag of coal, some firelighters and a box of matches with just two matches in it.

'She says we mustn't play with matches,' Abbas told us. 'So she emptied most of the matches out.'

'What does she think we are, babies?' asked Joe scornfully.

I agreed. Why would we want to play with

matches when we had all this to play with? We had a comfortable room, a blazing – well, smouldering – fire and best of all, the knowledge that we weren't going to be interrupted by a parent throwing open the door and saying something like, 'There's a documentary about dental hygiene on. Why don't we all watch it together?'

The fire was alight now and beginning to glow. We had hours of undisturbed viewing ahead of us.

'We could toast the bread if we had a toasting fork or something,' Abbas suggested.

'We've got one at home, I think,' said Joe. 'I'll try and bring it tomorrow.'

I could see I was going to have a lot of visitors.

'Ever tried toasted marshmallows?' asked Joe, who was now sunk deep into a bean bag. 'They taste really great.'

The fire blazed. I picked up the TV controls and flipped the channels. 'Who wants wrestling, "Neighbours" or MTV?' I asked.

The vote was for the wrestling. Terry the King Lawlor was behaving badly again.

'This is the life,' said Joe contentedly.

I had to agree.

CHAPTER FIFTEEN

Perfect Parents

No 8 Highfield Road became the favourite drop-in spot for Ian's drop-out friends. Most mornings I stepped over a sleeping body or two on the landing and stairs on my way to the bathroom.

One advantage of having the smallest bedroom was that it shared a wall with no 10, and Dad could wake me in the morning by thumping hard on the other side. This began after a few days of Helen, Ian and myself all oversleeping.

I'd get up and go straight round to no 10 – there was no hope of any breakfast appearing at no 8. Even though the fridge lost its protective plastic covering, the only food inside was for Helen and Harry. She had checked with Mum how to cook *boeuf en croûte*.

'Learn to cook beef before you try the *croûte*,'

was Mum's advice. She was torn between wanting to teach Helen to cook and her growing wish to poison Harry.

For an image consultant, he was very unpopular. He even managed to annoy our deaf neighbour by parking his flashy car in the alleyway that led to the back of our houses. The notes started arriving within days of our move. At first it wasn't clear what the note was about, since it was written in the shakiest handwriting I ever saw – on the back of a Christmas card.

When a Christmas card comes through the letter box in March, you've got to wonder.

'"Merry Christmas from Mabel and Jim",' Ian read out. 'Anyone know a Mabel and Jim? Helen, they sound like the people you mix with nowadays.'

'You mean the sort of people who don't feature in police files,' Helen snapped, snatching the card. 'The card's not for us. Someone's used it to write a note. Here it is, "Please don't park car in alley. It is causing ... causing ..." a something or other.'

Ian grinned. 'Harry's car,' he said smugly.

The Oily Rags had bought an old van, but kept it locked away in the guitarist's girlfriend's garage. It was cheaper than paying road tax.

'Dreadful lack of consideration,' tutted Ian, enjoying himself. 'Please ask Harry to be more considerate.'

'One doesn't want to upset one's neighbours,' I added.

At least our next-door neighbours were happy. Mum and Dad were thrilled about the two houses; they seemed to have solved everything. No 10 was neat and tidy from breakfast to supper and Mum and Dad pottered around like two little kids in a Wendy House. 'A place for everything, and everything in its place,' had become Mum's favourite saying, and Dad was trying his best to follow this.

'The Oily Rags sound quite tolerable when there's a few cavity walls between them and us,' Dad said cheerfully over breakfast one morning. We often chatted over breakfast now, instead of continuing the previous day's argument with Helen and Ian.

'Yeah, Ian's real pleased. He's got a

booking, well, sort of.'

'What do you mean?'

'He met Raw Meat and—'

'Just straighten your napkin, dear,' Mum interrupted. 'It's lying lopsidedly on your lap.'

'He met some raw meat!' Dad repeated, obediently straightening his napkin. 'Where do you do that – in a butcher's?'

Mum was hovering. 'Any more toast? Who can finish these last two sausages?'

'I can, thanks. Raw Meat – they're a thrash metal group. Styx's group. You know, Styx O'Connor. He used to sing in the choir with Ian.'

Mum leaned over to position the salt and pepper in the exact centre of the table. 'Little Martin O'Connor? He could reach High C,' she said. She piled two sausages and a leftover fried egg on my plate. 'I remember him.'

'Why's he called Sticks? Has he lost his legs?' Dad asked.

I groaned. 'Not that I've noticed. Anyway ... Raw Meat had double-booked, so they've offered the Oily Rags a gig.'

But Mum and Dad were wearing that haunted look that often came over them when the Oily Rags were discussed. I changed the subject.

'Sullivan's given me a place in the backs. I've got the speed to play forward, but he says he needs my strength.'

'Sullivan's your coach?' Dad was impressed. As a pupil at St Joe's, Tim Sullivan had played in the legendary '82 side, then gone on to play for Ireland. Now he was back as my history teacher and rugby coach.

'Wonderful!' said Mum. 'I'll have to feed you up. Anything more I can get you, dear? More toast?' She flicked at the table with a cloth. 'Please brush up those crumbs, dear.'

'Got any marshmallows?' I asked.

'For breakfast?'

'I want them for later,' I answered.

'I'll get some when I'm out shopping,' she promised, adding marshmallows to her shopping list which was kept in alphabetical order.

Thoughtful, considerate, caring. I had perfect parents for neighbours.

CHAPTER SIXTEEN

Triumph ...

'This is it!' announced Ian. He hadn't been so elated for ages, not since the days when a solo performance in the cathedral had been his idea of fun. He'd walked into my room without knocking, a grin plastered across his face.

'What happened?' I asked. It was Saturday morning and I was counting Great Uncle Albert's sock money, trying to decide how to spend it. The notes were laid out on the bed.

'Our first real gig tonight. An audience and a hundred quid! How does that sound?'

'Sounds fair. I'd listen to you for a hundred quid,' I said encouragingly, as I piled one tenner on another.

'They pay *us*. That's what they were going to pay Raw Meat. Styx's checking the address and phoning with the details. Make sure you get them right.'

'Where're you going then?' I turned to ask as Ian left my room.

'Got to pick up an amplifier. One of ours blew up,' he yelled over his shoulder.

'Well, I'm leaving in half an hour!' I shouted after him. 'I've got a big game today.'

But he was gone. 'Good Luck, David,' I muttered to myself.

Then Helen came in, shutting the door quickly behind her. 'What?' she asked.

'I'm wishing myself luck. I'm playing today.'

'What's that money?' Helen asked, ignoring the reference to rugby.

'Is this a quiz?' I asked, but Helen was listening for noises outside my room. 'What's up?'

'I've got a really important date with Harry. I need to get ready – and he's hovering out there ...'

'Psycho?'

'Yeah, he's going on about Doppelgängers.'

'What?'

'Doppelgängers, doubles. He says everyone's

got a look-alike. His is a street-seller he met in Tangiers. I haven't got time for his rubbish. I've got to wax my legs.'

'Spare me the details.' The phone was ringing. I shot out to answer it, passing Psycho who was loitering on the landing.

I picked up the phone in the hallway. 'Yeah?'

'Ian?'

'No, David.'

'Styx here. Tell Ian the gig's at–'

'Hang on, I'll get a pencil.'

'You can remember this. It's just Hell's Bells tonight, nine. Got it?'

'Got it.'

I ran upstairs, repeating the message, then grabbed a pencil. Leaning over the banisters, I wrote the message upside down on the wall above the phone: 'Hell's Bells nine'.

The plain white walls were proving useful. Already the wall by the phone was covered with numbers, details of homework I got from Joe or Abbas and messages for Ian (musical) and Helen (romantic).

By the time I'd listened to Psycho's theory

and let Helen into the bathroom, I was in danger of being late for rugby.

Ian returned, carrying an amplifier, just as I was leaving by the kitchen door, my rugby hold-all over my shoulder.

'Styx phone?' he asked.

'Yup.'

'So where are we playing?'

'The address is by the phone.'

He put the amplifier down and called through from the hall, 'This it – "Helmly Hotel, Foxrock"?'

'Yeah,' I shouted back, hardly listening. I was already focusing on the game ahead.

We had a long journey to St Mary's, our traditional enemies. If ever a school was mis-named, it was St Mary's. Huge, misshapen and vicious, their team was as determined to get through to the next round as we were.

'Look at the size of them,' complained Frazier, our captain, as the coach drew up and we gazed down at the opposition.

Sullivan, our coach, was ready with final words of encouragement, 'Remember, lads, it's not how big you are, it's how big you play.' That's why Sullivan was a great coach; he knew how to inspire the team. We were ready.

The first half of the game moved fast. Our superior speed was matched by their greater strength, so, by half-time the score stood at 16 : 14 to them. They were exhausted, we were battered.

Frazier had pulled a hamstring muscle and sat on the bench massaging it at half-time, an expression of pain on his face. Sullivan went over to speak to him, then turned to me.

'David, I'm moving you to no 8.' This was Frazier's position.

'Is Frazier going off?' I asked. The scowl on Frazier's face was answer enough.

'He's got to get that injury sorted out,' Sullivan said firmly. He patted me on the back. 'Abbas is coming on in the second row. What I want from you now is speed and accuracy.'

St Mary's started the second half well and increased their lead, but we came back, and, with five minutes of play left, there was again two points difference. The score was 23 : 21.

We were driving forward when the ball came back to me. Luckily the opposition thought the ball was still in the ruck – they'd missed the move. So I had time to try a drop goal. I took my chance. I kicked the ball. It soared and before it landed I heard yells of delight from St Joe's. It had sailed high over the bar; the score couldn't have been closer, it was 23 :24!

The whistle blew. St Joe's were jubilant.

'Through to the next round!' chanted Abbas gleefully. He'd got his opportunity to play in the A team and so had I. We'd won. Our chances of being picked again for the next game must be good. We were only two games away from the Cup Final.

'What a brilliant day!' I thought, as we made the long journey home.

Wrong again.

... and Disaster

As I walked up the hill towards our house, I saw the red BMW parked in the alleyway, but Ian's van was missing.

Inside was Harry, sitting on the edge of my sofa. 'I let myself in,' he explained, adding disapprovingly, 'The front door was ajar, the back door wide open and I found three downstairs windows unlatched.'

'We're trying to confuse the burglars,' I explained. 'Giving them a choice.'

'Where's Helen?' he demanded.

'How should I know? I've been playing rugby.'

'Hasn't she been in?' he asked, obviously agitated.

'I've been out!' I dumped my bag down on the white wool carpet, now a light grey.

'Wasn't she with you?'

He stared out of the window. 'She was,' he said tersely.

I flung myself on another sofa, picked up the controls and began rewinding my *Blackadder* tape. 'So what happened?' I asked wearily.

'Your brother turned up!' snarled Harry. He was dressed oddly in a dark suit with tails, a Fred Astaire without the footwork.

'Where?' I asked.

'At a wedding – the wedding of the year.'

I took another look at him. 'Who was getting married? You?'

'Don't be ridiculous, I was invited to Sean Connery's cousin's daughter's wedding. I was at school with the groom. It was going to be an excellent chance to meet people–'

'But you don't have to go to a wedding to meet people: the streets are full of them.' I was sitting like he was now, tensely.

'People who matter!'

'So what went wrong?'

'Ian and that group of his turned up. The Boil in the Bags or whatever they're called. They were already there when the guests arrived at the reception, playing some dreadful, fiendish racket.'

I leapt up. I'd heard Ian's van draw up outside and I knew I had just a few seconds to check. I rushed into the hall searching amongst the messages. 'Where was this reception?' I shouted back at Harry.

'Helmly Hotel, Foxrock,' he supplied.

Sure enough, on the wall, by the phone in Helen's small, neat handwriting was 'Helmly Hotel, Foxrock'. Ian had read Helen's message, not mine.

There was no time to clean it off. Helen was already storming through the front door, followed by Ian. 'I've never been so humiliated in my life,' she was saying. She pulled off her large brimmed hat and hurled it like a Frisbee at the stairpost.

'Yes, you have,' corrected Ian wearily.

I pointed towards the sitting-room, wondering how Helen had missed seeing Harry's parked car, but it became obvious that she knew he was there. She was just practising her temper on

Ian. She charged into the sitting-room and started on Harry. 'I do not appreciate your driving off without me.'

'Well, how do you expect me to react?' Harry replied. 'The bride's father was livid. He'd booked a nice quartet and five raving anarchists turned up.'

'Singer, keyboard, guitar and accordion, actually,' Ian whispered to me. We were standing, tactfully, I thought, in the hall. 'Music to grow old to.'

'Did the other lot turn up too?' I asked. There was no need to whisper now. Helen and Harry were both shouting so loudly even our deaf neighbour would be able to hear.

Ian nodded. 'We were on our third number when they arrived and tried to take over the stage. That's when the wedding cake toppled over.'

'One of the three-tier jobs? Brilliant.'

'... not quite the impression I wish to create,' Harry was shouting. 'One of my oldest friends arriving with his bride and your brother playing some—'

Ian put his head round the door. '"Angel of Death",' he supplied. 'We were playing "Angel of Death" when she walked in.'

Helen giggled, but Harry was as unsmiling as ever. 'I fail to see the joke,' he said pompously.

'You always fail to see the joke,' snapped Helen. She ripped off her pink elbow-length gloves, as if preparing for a fight. 'I'm fed up with this,' she began, as Mum walked slowly in from the kitchen. She must have heard the shouting, and had brought in a plate of cakes as an excuse to find out what was happening.

'I made these earlier,' she said brightly. 'Cherry rum cake, brandy snaps, coffee-frosted—'

'Harry's just leaving,' Helen interrupted, marching Harry to the door.

'Good riddance,' she muttered as the door slammed shut.

For a few minutes there was an atmosphere of tactful gloom. Then Mum asked hopefully, 'Is he gone permanently?'

That infuriated Helen. 'Mum, stop interfering!' she yelled. 'When will you realise that we want our independence? We don't want you coming round here interfering with ... everything.'

'I see,' said Mum, slowly and quietly. She put the plate down, just out of my reach and turned to face Helen. 'And what interference would you like me to cease? Cleaning your bathroom? Ironing your clothes?'

'Everything,' replied Helen, stooping down and picking up the cakes. The coffee frosted ones had thick, smooth icing, the crunchy brandy snaps were oozing cream.

'We're grown up now.' Helen continued as she thrust the plate back at Mum. 'We just don't need this sort of molly-coddling.'

'I see.' Mum was still unnaturally calm. 'Well,' she said, heading towards the back door, 'I shall respect your wish for independence. This is the last time I shall come in uninvited,' she added with an attempt at dignity.

I wanted to say something to cheer her up. I knew she was deeply hurt. I wanted her to know that I for one appreciated her attention, but she was moving fast towards the back door.

'... leave the cakes,' I managed, but the slam of the door drowned out my words. Mum had gone.

CHAPTER EIGHTEEN

Great Pretender

Harry had slammed out of the front door, Mum out of the back, and now Ian started shouting, 'So why did you send me to that hotel in Foxrock?'

'Me? I didn't.'

He dragged me into the hall to face the messages. 'Yes, you did. Here it is.' He pointed to, 'Helmly Hall, Foxrock' in Helen's loopy handwriting.

'That's not how I write. Look at it.' Helen had done everything but decorate the message with flowers.

I jabbed a finger at the message I'd written. 'Here it is. "Hell's Bells, nine."'

'So I'm meant to swing upside down to read

that? We're not all built like orang-utans.'

'Well, whatever species you're closest to, it's a pity you can't tell the time.'

'What?'

'You're meant to be playing in the Hell's Bells at nine. It's ten past.'

Ian was gone. Then the telephone rang.

'If that's Harry, tell him I never want to see him again and that he's the most pompous, affected, miserable, self-obsessed–'

Her voice followed me out the back door. I hadn't eaten all day, and was going in search of food.

❉   ❉   ❉

No 10 was so peaceful and quiet after all the yelling and slamming of doors at no 8.

'I played in the A team today,' I told Mum over my three-course dinner.

We were sitting in the kitchen, facing each other. Dad was obviously out, though Mum didn't mention him. 'That was nice.'

There was a long pause.

'Scored a goal from a drop kick.'

'Well done.' The quiet was starting to get eerie. I wasn't used to it.

I tried again. 'The goal that won the game.'

'Very nice.'

I tried a cheerful topic. 'At least Harry's got the heave-ho!'

'Let's hope so,' Mum answered, disappearing upstairs.

❋ ❋ ❋

Later, back at no 8, the phone was off the hook and Helen was deconstructing herself upstairs.

When she came down, she was transformed. At least three layers of colour and make-up had gone. She was wearing blue jeans, a Guns n' Roses T-shirt and her hair was covered by a scarf, gypsy style.

'Let's get out of here,' she said.

'Where do you suggest?'

Just then, Ian pushed the front door open. He was carrying an amplifier again.

'You're back early.'

'This one blew up too! We only played two numbers and the landlord refused to pay us.' He dumped the amplifier down on the greyish-white carpet. 'God, I hate music.'

'We're going out. Want to come?' asked Helen.

'Yeah, I know a few pubs we could go to.'

'But Dave's only twelve.'

'He looks sixteen.'

'I've been in pubs before. Don't worry – I won't drink. Sullivan'd kill me.'

Ian took his drum kit out of the van and left it in the hall, and we piled in. Out of nowhere came Psycho Phil, or his Doppelgänger, to join us.

'Know a great place,' he told us, guiding Ian to a pub I'd never noticed before.

'Karaoke tonight!' announced the notice outside.

'We're going in here?' asked Helen doubtfully.

'Yeah, why not?' Ian said.

'But you said you hated music.'

'Exactly.'

❀　❀　❀

The place was full and a girl had just finished singing 'Cinderella Rockafella'. I thought she must have been brilliant because the clapping and cheering was tremendous, but as the evening continued, I realised that applause was awarded for nerve not notes. Karaoke's like bungee jumping: you're admired for having the guts to do it. Neither is a musical activity.

Not, that is, until my brother went forward and took the microphone. He'd been drinking Fanta all night like me, so it wasn't Dutch courage that made him sing. He'd chosen the song carefully and he didn't need the words on the screen to prompt him.

He sang a Freddie Mercury hit, 'Great Pretender', and he sang every word as if he meant it.

When he finished, the applause was subdued. He'd sung it as well as Freddie Mercury, every note accurate, every line loaded with feeling. The audience was stunned. They'd come for Karaoke; they'd heard real music. The words, 'I'm pretending/That I'm doing well' kept repeating in my mind as we drove home. I knew the song was Ian's farewell to Heavy Metal. He was back with classical music.

Ian had got it right first time. By the time he was fifteen, he was tired of doing what Mum, Dad and everyone else expected, hence his Heavy Metal rebellion. Now he was facing up to the truth – he loved classical music. He wasn't going to pretend anymore.

Helen had worked it out too. Ian, at the wheel, was silent, but Helen turned to me and whispered, 'We've got Beethoven back.'

CHAPTER NINETEEN

The Fire Dims

Snow fell in April, throwing Dublin into chaos. The roofs of the houses in Highfield Road were covered in a rich thick layer like icing sugar.

Rugby practice was cancelled – not for our sakes, you understand, Sullivan would have *us* practising in a cyclone, but for the sake of the pitches.

Joe, Abbas and I slithered up the hill of Highfield Road and spent our spare time at no 8. We mastered the knack of toasting marshmallows (two seconds max, then they're crisp on the outside, soft inside). But by the time we perfected the toasting there was something wrong with the fire. I lit it every afternoon when I got home from school, using the thin wood from the dividing fence as kindling. And there was still coal left from before Mum's argument with Helen. But after nearly a month, the fire was slower and slower to light. Even when I got it alight, the coal produced more smoke than welcoming red glow.

Helen was worse than useless when consulted. 'Why isn't it lighting properly?' I asked her.

She gazed at the fire blankly. 'How would I know? Don't ask me. I've done enough for you,' she said bitterly.

I stared. I couldn't remember her doing a single thing for anyone else, let alone me.

'Just what have you done for me?' I asked sarcastically. I consulted my watch. 'Don't hurry. I've got five seconds. That should be more than enough time for a detailed list.' I'd heard her say this to Mum, years ago.

Helen narrowed her eyes at me just as Mum had done at her. 'You don't know how demanding it is running a house, David.'

'Running,' I laughed. 'Helen, you're not even walking this place.'

I looked around the sitting-room. One

curtain was hanging lopsidedly from its rail. The once white carpet was mottled with pink and grey sticky circles. Up in the bathroom, the towels had been emitting toxic fumes for days and the sink was growing a worrying mould on its grey rim. 'Running,' I repeated, 'the only thing running around here is bacteria.'

But Helen had slammed out of the room. I sighed. My conscience wasn't quite clear about the curtain rail. That might have come down during a fight that had developed between Joe and me, a fight that might also have been responsible for the splitting of one of the bean bags and the distribution of about a thousand plastic beans throughout the room.

Joe had been trying to strangle me with one of the curtains when Ian walked in – and this just goes to show how weird he is – ignored us completely. My older brother has never, not once, beaten anyone up on my behalf. Of course, with a physique like his he's not well-equipped to do much beating up. In fact, my brother would be more likely to reduce Joe to a quivering wreck by singing him an aria, which is almost what happened.

Ian just headed towards the piano, as if in a dream. Joe stopped strangling me and listened. He knew Ian had won a scholarship for his singing, but not that he could play the piano brilliantly. Ian began with 'Chopsticks', played with two fingers. As far as Joe was concerned, that's how everyone plays the piano.

But the 'Chopsticks' turned into some concerto or other which seemed to need a hundred fingers and Ian was playing the piano as if his life depended on it. Joe stared in disbelief. When the playing came to an end with a dramatic crescendo, he let out a slow whistle of appreciation.

'I never knew you could play like that,' he said admiringly.

'*That*,' answered Ian contemptuously, more to himself than to Joe. 'I want to play better than *that*.' And he started playing again.

From then on he was always at the piano, so often that it interfered with our TV watching. We tried turning the volume right up but it's very unnerving trying to concentrate with

Beethoven in the room with you. Even if we chucked marshmallows at him, he just kept on playing. Now, don't try to tell me that's normal behaviour.

CHAPTER TWENTY

A Mess

And then a terrible thing happened. The TV controls went missing. We searched the whole room for them, flinging the bean bags about so that the beans from the torn one flew in all directions, but we couldn't find the controls.

I challenged Psycho Phil who had turned up because he thought Helen would be home. 'You've taken the controls,' I said.

'Controls? What controls?'

'What controls? The supersonic jet controls. The border controls. The self controls. The TV controls, of course, you idiot.' I looked at Psycho. He was tall, but I've seen more muscle on a gerbil. I guessed that he weighed less than ten stone.

'Look,' I said. 'Try this. Stand up straight.' I got behind him but he swivelled round. 'No, stand that way,' I instructed, turning him back. 'Now, I'm going to catch you. Fall backwards.'

He didn't move.

'Just relax and fall backwards,' I repeated. I waited, ready to catch him. For a moment nothing happened. Then he crumpled to the floor in a faint.

Just then Ian walked in. He was strangely different. Gone was the razor blade in his left ear-lobe, back was the cherub-like expression. Stepping over Psycho, he headed towards the piano.

'Welcome home!' I said. 'Know what's wrong with the fire?'

But he just sat at the piano and started playing some intricate composition.

And still the fire wouldn't light properly. Joe didn't come round any more. Abbas did, but mainly to supply domestic advice from his mum. She couldn't speak much English so stayed in-doors a lot. I'd come to think of her, sitting inside, a Goddess of Domestic Science, waiting to hand out advice to me when I needed it. Abbas decided to consult her and report back.

It was bad news. 'She says how often do you clean it out?' he said.

'Clean it out? What do you mean "clean it out?" Coal burns, doesn't it?'

'Coal burns into ash,' Abbas pointed out, grinning. He pulled the front away from the fire grate. It was packed thick with ash.

'How do we get rid of this?' I asked Helen, who'd just entered the front room.

'No idea,' she said sharply. She was carrying a blouse. 'All this washing,' she moaned.

Mum still washed all my clothes at no 10, but she refused to do Helen's.

'You seem a bit ruffled today,' I said to her, grinning. 'In fact, you look positively unironed.'

Helen glowered. 'Friends round again,' she commented.

'At least my friends don't annoy the neighbours,' I retorted. We'd received another spidery note that morning written on the back of a 'Get Well' card.

We could read only two words: 'car' and

'blockage'. Helen had a new boyfriend, 'new' but not 'young'.

'If your boyfriends get any older, they'll be parking their Zimmer frames in the hall,' I commented.

Abbas looked uncomfortable. 'I'll go and get something to pick up the ash,' he offered, and sped off.

He returned with a small shovel that his mum said could be used for ashes.

I shovelled the ashes out from under the grate and into a plastic bag. The cinders left in the fire immediately began to glow red. But when I was carrying the bag of ashes out to dump them in the back garden, a funny thing happened. The plastic bag shrivelled to nothing and a mound of grey ash landed on the carpet.

'You idiot,' shrieked Helen. 'Look what you've done. Quick, quick! It'll burn the carpet.'

'Don't tell me what to do–' I began, but when Abbas started shouting, 'Where's the vacuum cleaner?' I realised there was a real danger of fire and I went in search of a vacuum cleaner too.

But we didn't have a vacuum cleaner. We

had a grand piano and a TV set as big as a Punch and Judy booth, but no vacuum cleaner.

'Get Mum's!' I shouted.

Helen ran next door. I kicked at the ash to stop it burning through the carpet. It was smouldering by now and some of the ash stuck like glue to the sole of my right shoe, which started to smoke.

I was just wiping that off on another bit of carpet when Helen returned with Mum. Mum had a bucket of water with her which she threw over the ash. There was a sizzle and then everything went silent.

Except Mum. 'Fancy even thinking of using a vacuum cleaner to suck up hot ashes,' she yelled. 'What did you think would happen when the fire met the electric current?' She was really livid. 'Or haven't you two heard of electricity?' she asked sarcastically.

'It was his idea,' said Helen, pointing to Abbas.

'Don't drag David's friends into this,' snapped Mum. 'You're meant to know what you're doing, remember?'

I did. Now look at Helen: she was the oldest, supposedly the most responsible of us, and she couldn't even organise this little place. I stared round the room. It was dismal. The ash had settled on every flat surface, adding an extra inch or two to the dust already there.

'This house is getting disgusting,' I complained.

Helen lifted her gaze from the wet ash and looked at Mum beseechingly. 'Mum?' she said.

Mum smiled in quiet triumph. 'This is nothing to do with us, is it?' she said sweetly to Abbas. 'Let's leave those who know how to run their own lives to it, shall we? Would you like a piece of oaty date cake, dear? Or would you prefer datey oat cake?' I heard her saying as she led Abbas out towards her back door. Since Mum got rid of her three children, she had the time to bake so many cakes that you'd think she was trying to compete with Mr Kipling.

Then I considered. 'Got rid of her three children' was pretty accurate.

I set about scraping up the soggy grey ash. Helen and Ian always went on about wanting more independence, but I didn't. Twelve years old and abandoned, I thought bitterly. Left to fend for myself with a sister intent on electrocuting the lot of us and a manic depressive brother.

The letterbox clicked. I picked up the card. On one side was a picture of two squirrels and a poem:

A birthday is a special day
For laughter, love and cheer
For sharing warm and happy times
With those you hold most dear.

On the other side was a scrawled message: 'Will call police if you park car in alley.'

Mum and Dad had a lot to answer for, I thought gloomily as I mounted the stairs to my cold, bleak bedroom.

The smell of burning lingered on the stairs and on the landing. That, and the realisation of my parents' criminal irresponsibility, made me feel sick.

CHAPTER TWENTY-ONE

Illness

After a restless sleep full of nightmares involving marshmallows, ash and fire, I woke and *was* sick.

'Helen!' I called feebly. I could hear the movement of jars and aerosols in the bathroom that signalled the beginning of Helen's day.

'Helen,' I shrieked, trying to combine feebleness with volume. 'I'm being sick.'

But Helen didn't reply. I felt so ill that I couldn't even waste energy on being resentful. Helen would be a dead loss as a nurse anyway. My head ached and my stomach heaved. I started thumping on the wall, hoping that Mum and Dad would hear. Nothing.

'Ian,' I tried. From the direction of Ian's bedroom came a sound that would have surprised me if I hadn't been preoccupied with my own sickness. It was the once familiar strains of Ian's violin. He was playing a beautiful melody, a lingering mournful tune. But I was being sick again.

Drastic action was necessary. I wrapped my dressing-gown around me and staggered down the stairs. My only hope was to reach no 10. There I would surrender myself to Mum and Dad's care and sympathy.

I pushed my way through the wet clothes and boots that blocked the back doorway. So much for Helen's ideas about uncluttered decor.

The cold air struck me as I slid on the encrusted snow. Despair hit me when I found the back door locked. Had Mum and Dad gone out? I had no idea what time it was. Perhaps they hadn't unlocked the house yet. I pushed my right shoulder against the door in a move similar to one that had crushed many an opponent on the rugby field, but in my weak state, the door seemed to push back at me. Silver sat snugly inside on the kitchen window sill, pretending that he didn't see me.

'Open this door!' I yelled. At last I heard the

beautiful sound of the door being unlocked.

'David.' Dad stood there in his pyjamas, looking shocked at my appearance. I barged into the kitchen and slumped at the table.

'Dad, I feel awful,' I complained.

Mum came downstairs and the Stirling Care and Rescue Service moved into action. I was led gently away to the spare bedroom, given lots of hot drinks and advice about how to get better. Even the advice was welcome after Helen and Ian's cruel indifference.

I've left a mess next door, I thought and smiled to myself as I slipped into sleep between the clean, well-ironed sheets.

CHAPTER TWENTY-TWO

Spend, Spend, Spend!

Over the next few days, while the snow melted, I was recovering from whatever it was I'd had.

'You could've picked up any number of germs in those ... unsanitary conditions,' said Mum with a shudder. 'When I went round to clean up your room, I saw some very strange mould in the sitting-room. It was pinky-grey with lumps ...'

'They'll have the Environmental Health Officer round next,' said Dad, winking at me, 'though a little untidiness is not a bad thing.'

Both Dad and Mum showered me with attention. Must be great, being an only child, I thought to myself. Here, in no 10, everything was cleanliness and order. There was a routine for everything, from lighting the fire to mealtimes. For instance, I realised how a blazing fire was regularly achieved. Every morning Mum would rake out the ashes, then put firelighters on crumpled-up newspaper in the grate, so the fire was ready to light later. She'd even put wooden fire screens in front of the fire, so everything was neat and tidy. Dream on, Helen!

I was unenthusiastic about returning to no 8. Ian and Helen were no fun to live with. By Saturday I was well enough to go next door and collect some of my belongings. I walked back into no 10 carrying a load of clothes and Great Uncle Albert's tall boy.

When Mum saw the statue she smiled. 'Come to stay then?' she asked.

I nodded. 'It's much better here,' I told her.

A visitor was sitting at the kitchen table, sampling the cakes.

'Here's someone we haven't seen for ages,' said Mum, delighted. 'Young Philip.' She sat down at the table and helped herself to a rum baba. 'I used to drive you to school when you were just this high,' she explained to Psycho Phil.

Like he's going to be impressed, I said to myself. Mum was treating him as if he'd been in Australia for ten years. She didn't seem to realise this was Psycho Phil who'd been dossing down next door and harassing her daughter. With my mum all you needed to do to get away with anything is to prove that you were once seven years old.

'So what are you doing now, Philip?' Mum asked brightly. Points, Leaving Cert, qualifications – parents' favourite topics were about to be discussed.

'I'm taking a year off,' grunted Psycho.

'Before university?' Mum guessed.

'No, between serial murders,' I said softly.

But Mum was off. 'Are you still interested in dinosaurs?' she asked.

'Every seven-year-old is interested in dinosaurs,' I pointed out, reaching for a butterfly cake. The way Psycho was putting the cakes away, there would be none left for me.

'I've decided to spend Great Uncle Albert's

money,' I told Mum, hoping to get her attention. 'I'm going shopping, I'm going to buy a camera tripod.'

But Mum was too deep in discussion about *Jurassic Park* to hear me. I grabbed another cake and left her to fuss over Psycho Phil.

I called into Abbas and we made our way to the shops. The tripod cost a mint, but it'd be worth it. I was going to make sure that from now on there would be records of our family's greatest moments.

On our way home we took a short-cut through a lane full of antique shops. As we passed one called Flanigan's I saw something in the window that made me stop and stare.

'Great Uncle Albert's ship!' I cried, pointing at the glass case in the centre of the window.

'What?' said Abbas, staring at the ship, but I couldn't wait. I was half-way into the shop, with Abbas muttering behind me, 'This place looks pricey.'

The antique dealer came out from a back room. He looked disappointed when he saw us.

'How may I help you?' he asked with exaggerated politeness.

'That ship, in the window,' I began. 'How much is it?'

'Ah yes, Venetian glass.' He didn't seem able to answer my question. He carried the dome out of the window and placed it on his desk.

I looked at it closely, remembering those times when I'd had to strain to look up at the ship on Great Uncle Albert's mantelpiece. 'There were tiny bubbles, I remember,' I said more to myself than anyone else, then explained, 'In my great-uncle's. He had one like this.'

The antique dealer began to look more sympathetic. 'Ah bubbles. Then that one was quite old. This one was made in – oh, probably about 1930.'

If it wasn't very old, it wouldn't be too expensive, I hoped. 'How much?' I asked again.

'Two hundred pounds,' he answered, without looking up.

'*Two* hundred pounds,' echoed Abbas. 'Well, that's that!'

I took out the rest of my money and counted

it out as the antique dealer and Abbas watched. 'Why do you want this if your uncle's got one like it?' Abbas asked, realising I was serious about buying it.

'That one disintegrated,' I explained. 'It was the best possession my great uncle had, apart from his medal.'

'A medal! What did he do to win that?' asked Abbas.

'I don't know. Nobody ever bothered to ask him,' I said indignantly. 'It was the George Cross,' I added.

The antique dealer looked up sharply. 'The George Cross – very impressive. Did you know that only a hundred or so were ever awarded?'

'What were they given for?' asked Abbas.

'For valour. A civilian would have to do something for which there was a ninety percent chance of his being killed to be awarded the cross,' he told us.

'You know,' he added, and his tone had changed, he was sounding quite human, 'I couldn't go below a hundred and fifty pounds for the ship. That's what I paid for it.'

'Well, would you keep it for me if I gave you this?' I held out the rest of my money. One hundred and ten pounds in crinkled ten-pound notes.

'Hang on.' Abbas held out seven pounds. 'You can have this towards it.'

I looked away, not sure what to say. He was a good friend, Abbas. He was the same on the rugby field: he gave one hundred percent.

'Thanks,' I managed.

The antique dealer took over. I suppose the sight of money had given him extra energy. 'Let's say, if I take this ...' he took the ten-pound notes, and ignored Abbas's proferred seven pounds, '... that you owe me thirty pounds. I'll keep the ship for you as long as you like.'

'A deal,' I smiled. I was getting the ship for one hundred and forty pounds. Abbas and I examined the glass ship as the antique dealer slowly and carefully wrote out a receipt for the money I'd paid him.

'They've got such detail,' said Abbas admiringly, pointing to the sailor-figures climbing up the glass rigging.

'And the colour,' I added. As far as I could remember every detail was identical to the original.

'And,' the antique dealer handed me my receipt, 'what happened to your relative's medal?'

'Lost,' I replied.

'A pity. A George Cross would fetch quite a sum at auction.'

'How much?' Abbas asked eagerly.

'Well,' the reluctance to say anything definite seemed to have returned. 'It depends on the citation of course, but one sold at Sotheby's for in excess of ...'

We waited.

'... ten thousand pounds.'

'Phew! Are you sure it's lost?' Abbas demanded.

'Sure,' I said. That the medal was worth a lot of money only confirmed what I had known anyway – that it was valuable. I felt that familiar sense of disappointment with my family. Why couldn't they be bothered to find out what Great Uncle Albert had done?

But then I looked at the glass ship which was,

in effect, mine, and that had been unexpectedly restored to me. I cheered up.

The antique dealer accompanied us to the door, seeing us out with a smile. 'Keep the receipt,' he advised with a friendly wave.

'He changed his tune,' commented Abbas as we walked idly towards Highfield Road.

'Money talks,' I replied. I felt pleased with my shopping, even though all I was taking home was the tripod.

'Come back to my place for tea,' I suggested to Abbas as we reached the hill.

He looked uneasy. 'Your place?'

'Not no 8,' I assured him. 'That's turned into a right dump. No 10, Mum's probably spent the day baking. We'll have a choice of about ten different types of cake.'

We hurried up the hill towards Highfield Road. 'I think I'll write to Great Uncle Albert's neighbour, see if she can tell me what he won the medal for,' I said.

I was thinking about this as Abbas and I entered the kitchen of no 10, just in time to see Mum hurling a cream meringue at Dad's retreating back.

Abbas muttered an excuse about getting home for tea and left, while I stared accusingly at Mum.

'What's happening?' I asked, putting down the tripod.

'Your father's infuriating,' yelled Mum, picking up cups and plates from the table and just thumping them down again in a different spot.

'What's he done?'

'I've told him a thousand times to put the spoon on the dish marked "spoon",' she continued.

'What spoon?' I asked.

'The spoon he stirs his tea with, of course,' answered Mum. 'And have you noticed the way he stirs his tea? Round and round and round. Anti-clockwise,' she added, as if anticlockwise was a crime.

'Really,' I said, reaching for my shopping. 'How terrible, anticlockwise.'

Mum sat at the kitchen table, staring miserably at the cakes. 'Oh, David, I know it's silly,' she wailed, 'but he's getting on my nerves.'

I had a strong feeling that I didn't want to hear this. 'He never used to,' I said sullenly.

'I know,' answered Mum. She'd started eating a meringue in a mournful sort of way. 'Dear Uncle Albert,' she said. 'He told me it was the same during the war.'

'The same as what?' I asked. She was definitely rambling and she was starting on another meringue.

'People were united during the war,' Mum replied. 'Like your dad and I used to be. And for the same reason, don't you see? Because we had a common enemy.'

I stared. 'You three,' Mum explained. 'Your dad and I never argued when we had you three to battle with!'

Charming! I thought as I dragged my tripod up to my room. Nobody was interested in hearing what I'd bought. The common enemy!

Over twelve years of tolerance and unselfishness and that was my reward?

CHAPTER TWENTY-THREE

A Blaze

I took refuge in Joe's house, even though it was a three-mile walk across the city.

It was dark by the time his mum hinted that I should be on my way. I set off gloomily for home. Back through the entire city centre, over O'Connell Bridge, across towards Highfield Road, I didn't pass one human being who looked as miserable as I felt.

I shivered. I tried imagining myself idling comfortably in front of a fire. But I couldn't picture where that fire was.

And then I saw it, straight ahead, glowing red against the darkening skyline – a bigger fire than the one I had imagined. Realising that it was in Highfield Road, I began to run up the hill.

The jangling of fire engines sounded behind

me. It's no 6, I thought. Obviously batty, the old lady must have made a bonfire of her Christmas cards and torched the whole house.

The sirens of two fire engines were deafening as they passed me.

Abbas, I thought, panting now as I tried to quicken my pace. Thick, dark smoke was clouding around the flames as I imagined Abbas's little brother setting fire to no 82 with a forbidden match.

Only when I caught up with the fire engines in Highfield Road did the most obvious explanation occur to me – Helen and Ian! Either Helen had tried to cook for some new bloke and flambéed no 8, or Ian's dodgy amplifier had been left plugged in and finally blown the electrics!

As the two fire engines joined the police patrol car outside the terrace, one thing was clear: it was nos 8 and 10 that were ablaze. An ambulance sped away, blue light flashing.

'Stand back!' shouted a fire officer, holding his arms wide to push us back from the heat of the fire.

I felt a hand on my shoulder. 'He's here!' It was Abbas's voice.

Then I saw Mum. 'Davy, Davy,' she cried, hurtling towards me. And Dad – just a bit more controlled. 'David, thank heaven you're safe!'

'Me? Why wouldn't I be?'

'We thought you were in no 8,' Mum explained.

Dad was shouting across to the fire officer over the crackling and spitting of the fire, 'He's here! We've got him!'

The officer ran towards us. 'That's everyone accounted for?'

'Everyone,' confirmed Mum, holding Silver in her arms.

'Helen and Ian! Where are they?' I asked.

'Helen's gone with Ian.'

'Where?'

'To the hospital.'

'Further back, please,' yelled the same fire officer at the growing crowd. We hurried across the street, turning back quickly as the roof of no 10 crumpled and fell.

In the confusion of sparks and falling roof-tiles, I was separated from Mum, Dad and Abbas. Frantically I searched for them, desperate to know about Ian.

I glimpsed Dad in the crowd. 'Dad!' I shouted. 'What happened to Ian?' The houses, the furniture, none of it mattered now. I just wanted to know my brother was okay.

I pushed through the crowd. 'Dad!'

He was staring at the fire as the burning staircase of no 10 finally collapsed. I shook him. 'Dad, is Ian burnt?'

He turned towards me, his face lit up by the flames. 'Ian's fine, David. Ian's a hero.'

CHAPTER TWENTY-FOUR

A Hero

Sleep's the last thing you want after a fire. Sleep would be like death, and when your home's burnt down, that's what you're happy to have escaped.

So I stayed with Abbas and we talked through the night, and Mum and Dad went off to Gran's.

First Abbas told me about Ian. 'The whole street knew there was a fire. Everyone shouted across the garden fences or hammered on doors, but no one remembered the old lady in no 6.'

The deaf old lady in no 6. I remembered how, before we moved in, Ian had regarded her deafness as a personal favour.

'Did Ian go in and rescue her?'

'Yeah. He was out when the fire started. He just drove up as we were leaving the house. And he ran straight into the house to get her.'

'Hang on. No 6 wasn't on fire!'

'She wasn't in no 6. She was in no 8. She was delivering something.'

A threatening note, of course.

'The front door was open and she'd gone in because she saw flames, then got frightened and confused by the smoke.'

'Obviously she didn't phone the fire brigade. So who did?'

'Helen, I think ...'

Ian was fine. He was taken to hospital for observation, because he inhaled a lot of smoke, but he wasn't hurt or burnt.

What impressed me was the way he chose to save the old lady rather than his violin. If he was lucky she'd recycle a 'Thank You' card to him for his courage.

Mum and Dad called round in the morning with the good news, Ian had been discharged.

Abbas's mum made Ceylon tea for us all while Abbas's little brother stood in the corner of the sitting-room watching us, his eyes wide. He'd been asking Abbas and myself hundreds of questions about the fire, but he was shy in front of Mum and Dad.

Mum tried to put him as his ease. 'Look at this,' she said, holding up a faded blue ribbon. At first I thought it was just something to get his attention, then I realised it was more important.

'Uncle Albert's medal,' I exclaimed.

'Yes,' Dad said.

I took it from Mum.

'It was hidden inside the tall boy. We found it yesterday when it ... er ... got broken,' Dad continued. So Mum hadn't stopped at throwing cream cakes.

I examined the medal. 'The George Cross,' I said admiringly. He must have risked his own life to get it. 'One day I'll find out just how he won it.'

'Actually, we know,' Dad said. 'He was in the Civil Defence Unit during the War. The munitions factory in Enfield was bombed and Uncle Albert pulled people from the collapsing building. He saved at least ten lives.'

'How did you find that out?'

'As soon as we found the medal, I made a few phone calls. You can check these things.'

'But I planned to write to that neighbour. I thought it would take ages!'

'David, has it ever occurred to you that some-one who's worked in Data Protection for twenty years might know where to enquire?'

It hadn't actually. 'So you managed to do all this and burn down two houses,' I said admiringly.

Mum and Dad looked shame-faced.

'Yesterday evening we drove around trying to find you,' explained Dad, 'but we couldn't.'

'Unfortunately ...' Mum began. Now she did look really ashamed. 'Unfortunately I'd rushed my chores that morning and set the fire with embers still hot from the day before.'

'While we were out the fire must have started up, set light to the wooden fire screens in front of it, and the whole lot went up,' Dad explained.

I shook my head, what irresponsibility. 'You

two make Psycho Phil seem normal.'

'Who?'

'Psycho, he's been haunting next door for months. You know, "dear little Philip". Six foot three, taking a year off. Slowing down from a dead stop.'

'Psy-*chic* Phil, you mean,' said Ian, coming in with Helen. '*Psychic*, we nicknamed him that after he predicted the winner of the Grand National.'

Abbas's mum had let Ian and Helen in. 'So this is the brave young man,' she said. 'You did a brave thing.' It was a long speech for her.

Ian blushed. He looked as shy as Abbas's little brother. 'Anyone would've done the same,' he muttered.

Both Mum and Dad looked at him in the way I remembered from when he used to win prizes and scholarships every week.

I felt proud of him too, but I knew he hated being the centre of attention. 'Pity Psychic Phil couldn't predict fires,' I said. It was the first distracting thing I could think of.

Dad smiled. 'The worst thing is that when we

came back and discovered both houses on fire, we blamed Ian and Helen,' admitted Dad.

'If the fire started in no 10, and you were out, who called the fire brigade?'

'I did,' said Helen.

'Thought so,' nodded Abbas.

'I had to run to a neighbour's though,' complained Helen, shaking as she remembered her panic. 'No 10 was locked. I couldn't make no 6 hear. I was frantic! I had to try four houses before I could dial 999.'

'Why didn't you phone from no 8?' I asked.

'Because Harry wouldn't get off the phone. He'd phoned me to say he was prepared to give me a second chance. The nerve of the man! As he was talking, I saw smoke billowing out of Mum and Dad's kitchen window. I put down the phone and tried to dial 999, but Harry hadn't put his receiver back. The line was engaged!'

'You did fine,' Dad said, hugging her. 'We're very proud of you.'

'Quick thinking for a beautician,' I said admiringly.

Mum sighed. 'We've learnt that our children are in some ways more responsible than we are.'

I felt genuinely sorry for her then. She looked so small and crumpled. She was crumpled because she didn't have a change of clothes, just like the rest of us, but from now on, to me, the smallness was permanent.

'Mum ...' I began. I wanted to explain that I appreciated her owning up. She'd made a mess of things, but at least she'd admitted it. That's not easy. But I couldn't find the words.

'You know the glass ship,' I began, irrelevantly.

'Uncle Albert's? Yes, I remember it.'

'I've found one just like it. I'm buying it.'

Dad stared. 'David, you really are a remarkable boy.'

Me – remarkable! The younger brother of a genius – remarkable!

Mum smiled in agreement. 'Thank goodness we've got you to keep the family together,' she said.

CHAPTER TWENTY-FIVE

Another Hero and Another Win

No 82 Highfield Road became the Stirling headquarters after the fire. 'This is a little house,' Abbas's mother said, 'but home for all our friends.'

So Mum and Dad arrived early on the day of the Cup Final just to drink Ceylon tea. 'So hospitable,' Mum said. 'They must be wonderful neighbours.'

My mind was on the weather. A bitter wind blew. When rain began to lash against the windows of Abbas's house just an hour before the game was to start, Mum said, 'I expect that nice Mr Sullivan will postpone the Final until the weather is better.'

'What?' I gave a hollow laugh and carried on

packing my gear. 'That "nice Mr Sullivan" would have us playing in a hurricane.'

I'd expected Mum and Dad to come and support St Joe's but when Helen got into the car, I was surprised. And when Ian got in too, I was staggered. 'This is a rugby match, not a concert,' I said.

'This is your big day. I'm coming to cheer,' he replied, without a trace of irony.

Then another figure squeezed into the back of the car. 'Psycho Phil,' I exclaimed.

'*Kick*, Psy-*kick*,' corrected Ian.

'Are we adopting him or what?' I asked.

'Leave the poor lad alone,' ordered Mum, Helen, Ian and I smiled – that's exactly what she would have said when she was driving a bunch of seven-year-olds to school.

Helen edged over and allowed Psy-*kick* Phil some space. We drove on towards school. But then we drove past the school.

'Shan't be a moment,' Dad reassured me. 'I just want to pick something up.'

That's not how it turned out though. Dad shot out of the car, having parked it on a double yellow line and given Mum instructions about driving off if a traffic warden appeared. But when he came back he was empty-handed.

'He won't give it to me,' he said to Mum. He added, 'David, come with me.'

He led me through the streets, past McDonald's and, as we headed down a side alley, I began to guess where we might be going. When he pushed open the door of Flanigan's antiques, I knew.

'Well, here he is,' Dad said triumphantly to the antique dealer.

'Is it the same boy?' asked the dealer. 'The other one was ...' He raised his arms in despair as an accurate description eluded him. I don't suppose he has many customers who turn up in hob-nail rugby boots.

'It's me,' I acknowledged.

'I expect he was more normal when you last saw him,' said Dad, adding unnecessarily, 'This is more his usual state.' He was counting out five-pound notes as he spoke.

The antique dealer took the wad of money and went into the back. He returned carrying the ship.

'Ah yes, I remember it now,' said Dad. 'I couldn't quite picture it. It's a work of art.'

The antique dealer handed the domed ship to me. 'I had to be sure it was the lad who'd paid the deposit,' he said, somewhat defensively.

'Of course, of course.' Dad had remembered the car on the double yellow line. He was keen to be away but, as before, money had loosened the antique dealer's tongue.

'Your uncle also had a George Cross, I remember.'

I was clutching the glass ship. It was quite a weight. I could only just see over the top of the dome. 'Yeah, that's right.'

'But you lost it.'

I nodded, but the nod was lost behind the dome. Fortunately Dad chipped in, 'Yes, but we've found it now.' He was heading towards the door, trying to avoid seeing or hearing the dealer's obvious enthusiasm.

Back in the car Mum turned to look at the ship on the seat beside me. 'You know. It really is beautiful,' she said with admiration.

'I know,' I said. 'I've always known.'

'I remember the other one, Uncle Albert's. I used to take it for granted. Something that was just there, taking up space.' She sighed heavily, and turned to look at Dad.

'Sometimes you have to look with fresh eyes to see beauty,' said Dad. He paused for a moment. 'You know, I think he wanted to buy Albert's medal.'

I had only ten minutes before my game started, but some decisions are easily made.

'Ian can sell the medal if he wants to,' I said.

There was silence. We were all thinking about how brave he'd been in the fire. The medal rightfully belonged to him. His violin had been destroyed in the fire and, if he was to get into the Royal Academy of Music as he now wanted to do, he'd have to replace both his piano and the violin.

'David, are you sure?' Mum asked.

It's difficult to made a dignified, noble gesture when you're wearing rugby shorts and you've got an antique ship resting on your knees, but I did my best. 'Yeah, I'm sure. He–' I began.

But Helen interrupted. 'Who's that cute guy

over there?' She shook her blond hair and smoothed it down. It was a gesture we knew and dreaded. She was wearing no make-up. That had been consumed in the fire, but she looked beautiful.

'Sullivan, my coach.'

'Introduce me.'

Families! I had a battle ahead of me and my sister expected introductions. I got out of the car, leaving Psychic holding the ship. I gave Ian a grin, then told Helen. 'Afterwards. Haven't got time now.'

The time for words had gone, Now my game had to do the talking.

Other books from
THE O'BRIEN PRESS

Also by Creina Mansfield

MY NUTTY NEIGHBOURS

After the strange events of *My Nasty Neighbours*, David and his family have moved from the city to the country – much to his disgust! David says: I'm telling you, there's nothing worse than living in the country. You think when people say 'the back of beyond' it's just a joke, but really it's a warning: Don't live here if you want to have a life! So here we are, the Stirling family, stuck in the  wilds. No one is happy – plus I'm pretty sure all country people are crazy. Could things get any worse?

From Vincent McDonnell

CHILL FACTOR

When Dr Denis Gunne disappears, the police believe he is fleeing charges of supplying drugs to addicts. His son, Sean is convinced that his father has been set up. But for what reason? With his friend, Jackie, Sean sets out to find his father. The trail leads to remote Fair Island where an American billionaire is forcing a team of scientists to work on a genetic project that could have 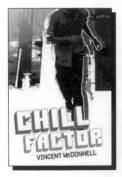 horrendous consequences for mankind. Can Sean rescue his father and thwart the evil plan?

From Oisín McGann

THE HARVEST TIDE PROJECT

Taya and Lorkrin are Myunans —
shape-changers who can sculpt their
flesh like modelling clay. They acciden-
tally release Shessil Groach, a timid
botanist working in captivity on the
top-secret Harvest Tide Project. A mas-
sive manhunt is launched by the sinister
Noranian Empire, which will stop at
nothing to protect its Project. With the
help of a scent-seller, a barbarian map-
maker and their uncle Emos, the teenag-
ers and Groach keep one step ahead of the Noranians,
while they try to find a way to sabotage the Harvest Tide
Project and avert the disaster it will unleash.

From Conor Kostick

EPIC

On New Earth, Epic is not just a
computer game, it's a matter of life and
death. If you lose, you lose everything; if
you win, the world is yours for the
taking. Seeking revenge for the unjust
treatment of his parents, Erik subverts
the rules of the game, and he and his
friends are drawn into a world of
power-hungry, dangerous players. Now
they must fight the ultimate masters of
the game — The Committee. But what Erik doesn't know
is that The Committee has a sinister, deadly secret, and
challenging it could destroy the whole world of Epic.

From Kevin Kiely

A HORSE CALLED EL DORADO

In the commune at the edge of a forest in
Colombia, life is blissful. Until the
guerrillas come. Then Pepe must flee
with his mother to the city, leaving
behind his favourite horse, El Dorado.
Hi future looks grim until his Irish
grandparents offer him another chance.
But can thirteen-year-old Pepe go all on
his own to this strange, cold land, the
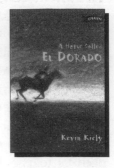
birthplace of his father? And what future awaits him there?
Will he ever have the chance to ride his beloved horses
again?

From Deborah Lisson

TRUTH SEEKER

A young Viking boy flees his homeland
and cruel stepfather to join his real father
– a legendary warrior living in Dublin.
His ambition is to gain honour through
battle and brave deeds, using his
powerful sword, the Truth Seeker. But
he soon learns that not all battle is
glorious, not all death honourable, and
that sometimes your enemies have as
much to teach you as your own people.

A powerful coming-of-age story, set against the turbulent
background of Viking raids, feudal battles and the bloody
demands of the god Odin.

From John W. Sexton

The Johnny Coffin Diaries

Twelve-year-old Johnny Coffin is a drummer in a band called The Dead Crocodiles, goes to school with the biggest collection of Murphys in the whole country, and has a madcap girlfriend, Enya, who has a man-eating pet. In his diaries Johnny chronicles his problems with acne, isosceles triangles and his teacher, Mr McCluskey, who is trying to destroy his mind with English literature.

Johnny Coffin School-Dazed

A shooting star flashes over the town of Kilfursa and Johnny Coffin makes a wish. That's when the trouble starts. Strange lights follow the school bus, hedgehogs throw themselves at the traffic and all the town dogs go missing. Enya's pet crocodile has also disappeared and Enya wants it back, NOW. Their teacher, Mr McCluskey, becomes totally unhinged. And the homework he's setting in class becomes weirder and weirder. Is it any wonder that Johnny and his mates are school-dazed? And there's definitely *something* out there ...

Send for our full-colour catalogue or check out our website

www.obrien.ie